*From the Pages of*
# SIDDHARTHA

Siddhartha had a single goal before him, one and one only: to become empty, empty of thirst, empty of desire, empty of dreams, empty of joy and pain. To die away from himself, no longer to be I, to find the peace of the emptied heart, by thinking away from the self to stand open to the miraculous: this was his goal.     (page 13)

"This has nothing to do with opinions, they may be lovely or hateful, clever or idiotic, each of us can hang on to them or dispense with them. But the teachings that you have heard from me are not opinion, and their goal is not to explain the world to those who hunger for knowledge. They have another goal: their goal is deliverance from suffering."     (page 29)

I have still not seen a human being look or smile, sit or walk that way, he thought; I, too, wish to be capable of gazing and smiling so truly, of sitting and walking so freely, so venerably, so cryptically, so openly, so like a child and full of secrets.     (page 30)

He looked around, as if he were seeing the world for the first time. The world was beautiful, the world was particolored, strange and quizzical. Here was blue, here was yellow, here green, the sky flowed and the river, the forest froze with the mountains, everything beautiful, everything full of mystery and magic, and in its midst he, Siddhartha, the awakening one, on the way to himself.     (page 34)

Now he was only Siddhartha, the one who had awakened, nothing more. Deeply he drew in his breath and for a moment he froze and stood shuddering. No one was as alone as he.     (page 36)

She drew him toward her with her eyes, he inclined his face toward hers and lay his mouth on her mouth, which was like a freshly split-open fig. For a long time he kissed Kamala, and Siddhartha was filled with deep astonishment as she taught him how wise she was, how she ruled him, put him off, lured him back, and how behind this first row of kisses came another long, well-ordered, well-tested series, each one different from the other, still awaiting him. Breathing deeply, he remained standing and at this moment he was like a child astonished by the abundance of knowledge and things worth learning opening up before his eyes.          (page 48)

"Anyone can work magic, anyone can reach his goals, if he can think, if he can wait, if he can fast."          (page 50)

"Most people, Kamala, are like falling leaves, which blow and turn in the air, and stagger and tumble to the ground. But others, fewer, are like stars, they travel in a fixed orbit, no wind reaches them, in themselves they have their law and their course. Among all the scholars and shramanas, of whom I knew many, was one of this type, a Perfect One, I can never forget him. That is the one called Gautama, the Exalted One, the prophet of the teachings. A thousand disciples hear his teaching every day, every hour they follow his precepts, but they are all falling leaves, in themselves they do not have the teachings and the law."          (pages 59–60)

"I have lost my riches, or they me. They are out of my hands. The wheel of forms turns quickly, Govinda. Where is Siddhartha the Brahmin? Where is Siddhartha the shramana? Where is Siddhartha the rich man? Quickly the mutable changes, Govinda, you know that."          (page 74)

And if Siddhartha listened attentively to this river, to this song of a thousand voices, if he did not listen to the pain or the laughter, if he did not bind his soul to any one voice and enter into it with his I, but rather listened to all, the entirety, perceiving the unity, then the great song of the thousand voices consisted of one single word, and the word was *OM*: perfection.          (page 106)

# SIDDHARTHA

## An Indic Poem

HERMANN HESSE

*Translated from the German by Rika Lesser*

*With an Introduction and Notes*
*by Robert A. F. Thurman*

George Stade
Consulting Editorial Director

BARNES & NOBLE CLASSICS
NEW YORK

## BARNES & NOBLE CLASSICS

### NEW YORK

Published by Barnes & Noble Books
122 Fifth Avenue
New York, NY 10011

www.barnesandnoble.com/classics

The two parts of *Siddhartha* were first published together in book form in German in 1922 by S. Fischer Verlag. Rika Lesser's new translation is based on this 1922 edition.

Published in 2007 by Barnes & Noble Classics in paperback in a new translation and with a new Introduction, Translator's Note, Notes, Biography, Chronology, Inspired By, Comments & Questions, and For Further Reading.

*Siddhartha*
ISBN-10: 1-59308-379-3
ISBN-13: 978-1-59308-379-3
LC Control Number 207927680

Produced and published in conjunction with:
Fine Creative Media, Inc.
322 Eighth Avenue
New York, NY 10001

Michael J. Fine, President and Publisher

Printed in the United States of America

QM

19   20   18

# HERMANN HESSE

Hermann Hesse was born on July 2, 1877, in Calw, Germany, to a family of Pietist theologians and missionaries. His grandfather, Hermann Gundert, and his father and mother, Johannes and Marie Gundert Hesse, had lived and worked as missionaries in India. By the time Hesse was born, his parents had settled back in Europe, where they divided their time between Calw and Basel, Switzerland, headquarters of the Pietist movement.

Hesse was a good if somewhat inconsistent student. He attended preparatory school in Göppingen and easily passed the notorious Swabian state examination, which made him eligible to study for the Protestant ministry at the prestigious Maulbronn Seminary. He was unhappy at the seminary, however, and ran away after less than a year. Seriously depressed, at age fifteen he attempted suicide and spent a brief period in an institution. Finally, he enrolled in secondary school at Bad Cannstatt, where he finished his formal education. Hesse spent a year apprenticing with a clockmaker in Calw, and then moved to Tübingen, where he worked as a book dealer. In 1899 he moved to Basel, Switzerland. The same year saw the publication of his first works, the prose collection *An Hour Behind Midnight* and a volume of poetry, *Romantic Songs*. Hesse achieved literary success in 1904 with the publication of his first novel, *Peter Camenzind*. He married in 1904, and the couple settled in the small German town of Gaienhofen, near the Swiss border. A trip to the East Indies in 1911 marked the beginning of Hesse's deep interest in Eastern religions and cultures, and motivated him to write *Siddhartha*.

By the start of World War I in 1914, Hesse had moved to Bern, Switzerland. Although he initially volunteered (and was rejected) for military service, as the war progressed he grew increasingly critical of widespread German nationalism, a stance that made him unpopular among his neighbors. This period was also marked by personal depression and stress, brought on by the death of his father, his failing marriage, and the illnesses of his wife and son. In 1916 Hesse underwent psychoanalysis with J. B. Lang, a student and assistant of the renowned Swiss psychiatrist Carl Jung. After the war, Hesse left his family, settled in Montagnola in southern Switzerland, and entered the period of his greatest works, including *Demian* (1919), *Siddhartha* (1922), and *Steppenwolf* (1927).

With the end of the Weimar Republic and the rise of Nazism, Hesse's works, some of which addressed anti-Semitism, were banned in Germany, and after the publication of *The Glass Bead Game* (1943) he was blacklisted by the Nazis. Throughout World War II, Hesse continued to denounce German atrocities from his home in Switzerland. His collection of political essays entitled *If the War Goes On . . .* was published in Zurich in 1946.

Many of Hesse's major works, including *Siddhartha*, *Rosshalde*, and *The Glass Bead Game*, were not introduced in the United States until the 1950s and 1960s. They were immensely popular, and Hesse became something of a prophet to American Beat writers such as Ken Kesey and William Burroughs, Jr. He was awarded the Nobel Prize for Literature in 1946; in his acceptance speech he expressed kinship with "the idea that inspired the Nobel Foundation, the idea that the mind is international and supra-national, that it ought to serve not war and annihilation, but peace and reconciliation." Hermann Hesse died from a cerebral hemorrhage on August 9, 1962.

# CONTENTS

The World of Hermann Hesse and *Siddhartha*
IX

Introduction by Robert A. F. Thurman
XIII

Translator's Note
XXVII

*SIDDHARTHA*
1

Notes
119

Inspired by *Siddhartha*
133

Comments & Questions
135

For Further Reading
139

# The World of Hermann Hesse and
# SIDDHARTHA

**1875** Swiss psychiatrist Carl Gustav Jung is born in Kesswil, Switzerland.

**1877** Hermann Hesse is born on July 2 in Calw, Germany, to a family of Pietist missionaries. (A movement within the German Lutheran Church, Pietism stressed personal piety and devotion.) His parents—Johannes Hesse, originally from Estonia, and Marie Gundert Hesse, of German and French-Swiss descent—earlier lived as missionaries in India. During Hesse's childhood, the family lives in Calw and in Basel, Switzerland.

**1890** Hesse attends grammar school in Göppingen, where he excels in the study of Latin. In July he passes the Swabian state examination, a prerequisite for studying at exclusive Protestant ministry schools in Württemberg, Germany.

**1891** Hesse enrolls in the theological seminary at Maulbronn, in Württemberg.

**1892** Depressed and unhappy at the Maulbronn seminary, Hesse runs away. His parents place him in secondary school in Bad Cannstatt.

**1894** Hesse's formal education ends; he becomes a mechanic's apprentice at Heinrich Perrot's tower-clock factory in Calw.

**1895** He moves to Tübingen, Germany, and works as a book dealer. Determined to become a writer, he spends his free time reading and writing.

**1899** He moves to Basel, Switzerland, and finds work in a bookshop. His prose collection *Eine Stunde hinter Mitternacht* (*An Hour Behind Midnight*) and his first volume of poetry, *Romantische Lieder* (*Romantic Songs*), are published but go largely unnoticed.

**1901** Hesse writes articles and reviews for German journals.

**1904** His novel *Peter Camenzind*, about a failed writer, is published to great success. He marries Maria Bernoulli, and the couple move to Gaienhofen on Lake Constance, in Germany near the Swiss border. Hesse is awarded the Bauernfeld Prize.

1905    His first child, Bruno, is born—followed by Heiner in 1909 and Martin in 1911.

1906    *Unterm Rad* (*Beneath the Wheel*) is published.

1910    *Gertrud* (*Gertrude*) is published.

1911    Hesse travels to Sumatra, Borneo, Singapore, Burma, and Sri Lanka. He begins to study Eastern religions, particularly ancient Hinduism, or Vedism, and Buddhism, which will profoundly influence his later writing.

1912    Hesse and his family move to Bern, Switzerland. Jung publishes *The Psychology of the Unconscious: A Study of the Transformations and Symbolisms of the Libido*; initially an ardent supporter of the work, Hesse will later grow critical of it.

1914    *Rosshalde*, in which Hesse explores the question of whether an artist should marry, is published. World War I begins; Hesse volunteers for military service but is rejected. He works for the Prisoners of War Welfare Organization in Bern, providing German prisoners of war with books. Throughout the war he is increasingly critical of widespread militaristic sentiment and nationalism in Germany, and is ostracized by his neighbors.

1916    Under tremendous mental stress brought on by the death of his father and the illnesses of his wife and son, Hesse undergoes psychoanalysis with Jung's student and assistant J. B. Lang.

1918    World War I ends with Germany's surrender to Allied forces on November 11.

1919    A democratic, more centralized federal constitution is adopted at Weimar, and Germany becomes known as the Weimar Republic. Hesse joins in the effort to rebuild postwar Germany by coediting *Vivos Voco*, a journal aimed at educating young people. He separates from his wife, Maria, and leaves Bern for the small town of Montagnola in southern Switzerland. His novel *Demian* is published under the pseudonym "Emil Sinclair," the name of the novel's narrator; it receives high praise from German novelist Thomas Mann, who compares it to James Joyce's *Ulysses* and André Gide's *The Counterfeiters*. Hesse falls in love with Ruth Wenger, daughter of Swiss writer Lisa Wenger.

**1920** *Blick ins Chaos* (*In Sight of Chaos*), a collection of essays, is published.

**1922** *Siddhartha*, a novel reflecting Hesse's immersion in Asian mysticism, is published. Hesse dedicates *Piktors Verwandlungen* (*Pictor's Metamorphoses*), a fairy tale, to Wenger.

**1923** In July his divorce from Maria is finalized.

**1924** Hesse is granted Swiss citizenship. He marries Ruth Wenger. The first English translation of *Demian* is published.

**1927** Hesse and Wenger divorce. *Der Steppenwolf*, in which Hesse sensationalizes the *doppelgänger* (double, or alter ego) phenomenon, is published.

**1929** *Steppenwolf* is translated into English.

**1930** *Narziss und Goldmund* (*Narcissus and Goldmund*), a novel set in medieval times, appears.

**1931** In November Hesse marries his third wife, Ninon Dolbin-Ausländer, a Romanian Jewish art historian with whom he has corresponded since 1909. He begins work on *Das Glasperlenspiel* (*The Glass Bead Game*), a novel that many consider his masterpiece.

**1932** *Die Morgenlandfahrt* (*The Journey to the East*) is published. *Narziss und Goldmund* is translated into English as *Death and the Lover*.

**1933** The Weimar Republic falls, and Nazism is on the rise. On January 30 Adolf Hitler is appointed chancellor of Germany; on March 23 he is given full dictatorial powers by the German Parliament. In May a book-burning campaign begins in Berlin and spreads throughout Germany.

**1934** Hesse becomes a member of the Swiss Club of Poets, an organization established to protect German writers from Nazi policies.

**1937** Hesse's autobiography, *Gedenkblätter* (*Reminiscences*), is published. An official circular is printed in Germany to defend Hesse's works from attacks.

**1939** World War II begins.

**1941** With the 1941 reprinting of *Narcissus and Goldmund*, Hesse refuses to censor parts of the book that deal with anti-Semitism.

**1942** He sends the manuscript of *The Glass Bead Game* to Berlin but is refused publication.

**1943** A Zurich publisher issues *The Glass Bead Game*. Hesse is placed on the Nazi blacklist.

**1946** After the war, Hesse retreats from public life and lives in seclusion in his home in Montagnola. He is awarded the Nobel Prize for Literature and the Frankfurt Goethe Prize. *Krieg und Frieden* (*If the War Goes On . . .*), a collection of political essays, is published in Zurich.

**1951** *Siddhartha* and *The Journey to the East* are translated into English; the two works become immensely popular with American Beat writers, including William Burroughs, Jr., and Ken Kesey.

**1952** *Gesammelte Dichtungen*, a complete edition of Hesse's works, is published in six volumes.

**1955** Hesse receives the Peace Prize of the German book trade. *Beschwörungen* (*Evocations*), a volume containing his later prose, is published.

**1958** A second English translation of *Demian* is published.

**1961** Austrian Nazi Adolf Eichmann is hanged for his crimes against the Jewish people and humanity. *Peter Camenzind* is translated into English.

**1962** Hesse dies of a cerebral hemorrhage on August 9 in Montagnola.

**1970** *Rosshalde* is translated into English.

**1972** The Hollywood film version of *Siddhartha*, directed by Conrad Rooks, is released.

**1974** Fred Haines's film version of *Steppenwolf*, starring Max von Sydow, is released.

# INTRODUCTION

Hermann Hesse's *Siddhartha* is a great story, a tale of a gifted individual struggling to discover the meaning of his life. Through his many colorful adventures, he does not settle for conventional answers, but experiences the whole range of human possibilities for himself and comes finally to profound insight and vast compassion.

The story brings to life a human being's arduous quest for enlightenment, and has a strong resemblance to the story of the historical Buddha, Shakyamuni. Hesse intends it to echo the life of the Buddha: He gives the hero the auspicious name Siddhartha, which was Shakyamuni Buddha's name when he was still the crown prince of the Shakya nation, before he awoke to Buddhahood. On top of that, Hesse sets his story in the same time and has Siddhartha meet, at a critical moment in his quest, Shakyamuni Buddha himself in all his glory. Siddhartha has gained enough insight by this time to recognize a buddha—"an awakened one"—and he feels overwhelmed with joy. He is inspired by the World Teacher and admires his liberating presence. Unstinting in the reverence he lavishes on the Transcendent One, Hesse is unusual for European intellectuals of that era, who tended to fear the Buddha, confusing him with a world-negating nihilist. Then, there is a twist to the plot that in its artfulness is characteristic of the author: Siddhartha honors the Lord of Bliss by *not* following him, by not taking refuge in the new community of seekers of the liberating truth. Leaving his lifelong friend Govinda under the Master's care, Siddhartha meets with the Buddha and respectfully announces that he will seek the supreme fulfillment of enlightenment on his own. Hesse catches the deep point that the enlightenment of the Buddha, of Siddhartha, or of anyone, must be original—that is, brought up from deep within the individual, by the individual.

Nowadays there are endless textbooks introducing us to "Buddhism," as well as learned and ever more accurate translations of important texts from within the many Buddhist traditions themselves. I produce these kinds of works myself. But *Siddhartha* is a work on a different level. It is great art. It moves the heart. It tells a story. It brings the great issues of life and death to within our experiential reach. Hesse himself lived through the inner changes required on such a path. He refined his sufferings and his joys in the crucible of art, and thus he brings the path to life in our hearts. Written nearly ninety years ago, *Siddhartha* is still fresh and moving and illuminating.

Through a deep engagement with India, Hesse, a gifted yet troubled German-born poet from a European, Christian missionary family, dramatized his understanding of the Buddha, India, and the universal search for personal meaning, happiness, and perhaps even some sort of supreme enlightenment. He wrote at the moment when Europe was absorbing the fruits of centuries of imperial conquest of the planet, fighting over the spoils, so to speak, in World War I. After an initial knee-jerk patriotic reaction to the war, Hesse turned away from it and gradually became dedicated to nonviolence, even as Gandhi was developing his own understanding and practice of nonviolence in South Africa and then India, long before he was well known. Further, just before and during his writing of *Siddhartha* in 1918 and 1919, Hesse was in the midst of a profound outer and inner crisis. His family had broken up: His wife had been institutionalized, his three sons had been placed under the care of relatives and friends, and Hesse had fled from their residence in Bern in northern Switzerland to take refuge in the southern town of Montagnola, in the idyllic Swiss-Italian region of Ticino. He visited Zurich on the way, seeking spiritual and psychiatric help from the great Carl Jung.

Hesse presents in *Siddhartha* a prose-poem of lived philosophy, expressing a deep personal search for the transcendent yet experienced meaning of life. It is a gripping human drama of fathers and sons, lovers and ascetics, and it introduces the West to the possibility of the transcendent wisdom of the Buddha. In Hesse's time, in the heart of Europe, only a tiny number of people would even entertain the idea that there is such a thing as a truly higher consciousness, a kind of higher intelligence that makes conventional awareness seem like being asleep. To Westerners, a step in the right direction to "enlightenment" meant awakening from mental imprisonment in dogmatic religion. It meant secularism; manipulative rationality; science as the systematic measurement of all dimensions of the physical universe; and above all, materialism. The possibility that there is another, deeper enlightenment, one that is experiential as well as intellectual, spiritual as well as scientific, transcendentally stable and yet consciously evolutionary, blissful, loving, humorous, and earthy—such a state of being accessible to humans was unheard of and unimaginable. It was first of all Hesse who made such a possibility—a conscious human evolution upward into higher dimensions of awareness—seem real to the Western public, by dramatizing it.

Still today, materialism is far too prevalent, challenged only by a kind of regressive fundamentalism that in turn stiffens the resolve of the secularists to remain opposed to all spirituality. The path to enlightenment still needs to be brought forth to the imagination as a living possibility, as Hesse did so vividly nearly a century ago.

Given how much less scholars knew about the "inner sciences" of the East in Hesse's time, it is astonishing how accurately Hesse intuited the foundational individualism of the quest for enlightenment. He focuses on this individualism as a transcendent good, yet at the same time does not abandon the exalting taste of the selfless love of life and humanity. His tale is an evocation of the lush beauty of nature, an enrichment of the mystical aestheticism of Europe with the timeless earthiness of India.

I first read *Siddhartha* at the very start of the 1960s, and I can still remember the powerful inspiration it gave me. Why would a young person seeking to escape from WASP-hood at Harvard turn to India as the mother of inner exploration, when nothing in Western education would indicate that India was a source of great explorations in the quest for some transcendent truth? Clearly, Siddhartha was a model for my own journeys, for my own development of his vaunted skills at "fasting—waiting—thinking."

Looking into Hesse's personal life, I was astonished to discover many parallels between the troubled youth of this great psychic explorer, poet, critic, novelist, painter, and gardener who wandered the world before World War I and finally fled from the Rhineland down to southern Switzerland, and that of my own more humble and less accomplished self, hailing from Manhattan and traveling more or less on foot to India my first time out in 1961. At fifteen Hesse began to rebel against his strict Pietistic father and mother and the mission school they placed him in; he never felt comfortable in conventional German society of the time. Some of us—certainly myself, and I think Hesse, too—though born in the West, tend to wander as if doomed to exile and always feel like "a stranger in a strange land." For both of us, forty-plus years and another World War apart, "Mother India" was a salve, a home, for our wandering spirits. Why? Is it because India's civilization alone has had the wisdom to open itself up truly to embrace the naturally homeless? Hesse himself had this to say about India:

> For example, with my Indian journey I had an unforgettable experience. At first it was a real disappointment, I returned completely downcast. But almost ten years later, as I was writing *Siddhartha*, suddenly the Indian memories were extremely precious and positive, and the little disappointment of earlier on was extinguished.*

*Siddhartha* was published in German in 1922. Its first English translation was published in 1951. Siddhartha's quest was an important model for the whole postwar generation's seeking of "Enlightenment in the East." For Hesse himself, the book articulates a complex of strands in his character. It shows his rich appreciation for India conceived in a specific Western way, inherited from his missionary grandfather and parents. He says:

> And this learned and wise grandfather had not only Indian books and scrolls, but also shelves full of exotic wonders, not only coconut shells and strange birds' eggs, but also wooden and bronze idols and

---

*All quotations from Hesse are drawn from the English version of "Documentation of the Permanent Exhibition, Museum Hermann Hesse, Montagnola." Visiting that museum, which is near Lugano, Switzerland, was a revelation, like a meeting with Hermann in person, in his favorite landscape.

animals, silken paintings and a whole cabinet stuffed with Indian cloths and robes in all materials and colors.... All this was part of my childhood, not less than the fir-trees of the Black Forest, the Nagold river, or the Gothic chapel on the bridge.

*Siddhartha* is distinguished by Hesse's consummate artistic, spiritual, and poetic sense of the high transcendent experiences and values accessible through the Indian "inner sciences" and "mind yogas." At the same time, the book contains a certain European, world-weary cynicism and a sense of the inevitable faultiness of all religious paths. Hesse again: "At the age of thirty, I was a Buddhist, of course not in the church-sense of the word." The book hums with Hesse's pursuit of Christian, Tolstoyan nonviolence and the inner kingdom, all the while roiled from within by its opposite: his own driving inner violence, his volcanic sensuality, and his deep despair of fulfilling human relations—a despair that stemmed from his ambivalent struggles with his parents and his ups and downs with his first wife and three sons.

Rereading *Siddhartha* now, I can clearly see its influence on my decision at twenty to leave college and the study of Western literature, philosophy, and psychology, and seek a higher enlightenment in India. More than forty years later, I have gone back and forth from "the West" to "the East" so many times I can hardly tell the difference anymore, though I observe certain groups still struggling to maintain the "never the twain shall meet" sort of attitude. Having trod a little bit in both of the Siddharthas' footprints in my own small way, I appreciate the book even more. I can now unravel the tangled threads of Hesse's mixing of Hindu and Buddhist worldviews, his entrapment in some of the stereotyped views of "the East" that were almost inescapable for a man of his time and culture, and his romantic depiction of Buddhist/Hindu enlightenment as a kind of return to nature, a resignation to the flow of the great river of life. In spite of this creative Hindu/Buddhist mixing, I enjoy the book much more now than I ever could have in my youth.

Hesse seems to have been haunted by a keen insight into the human condition, and his work seems to mark a great turning point in the growth of a genuine European respect for the civilization of enlightenment that developed in ancient India. He himself loved nothing more than to leave hearth and home and wander south to Italy with artistic friends, the European version of a *sadhu* (Hindu ascetic). He slept in bed-and-breakfasts or camped alfresco, contemplated nature and art, and took a break from the routine chores of householding in northern Europe (very likely overburdening his high-strung wife with their three sons). But it was hard to wander with open mind and heart and intellect in the Europe of that time, so he also went to the East Indies and southeast Asia. His keen artist's perception saw there that the complex fabric of the culture of India was rich enough and its weave loose enough to accommodate all manner of eccentrics, wandering here and there, always on some spiritual pilgrimage or other, seeking beauty or peace, magical energy or complete transcendence.

At this moment in my journey, I am very pleased to have the chance to introduce *Siddhartha* to a new generation, since I think it still has the power to inspire the seeker of higher truth. I do not pretend to evaluate Hesse's great achievement from some higher vantage of supposed enlightenment, which I do not claim for myself. But I have put in a bit of study of enlightenment's various forms and levels, the institutions and cultural orientations it has supported in various countries, and the high civilizations it ultimately created. And following Siddhartha's inspiration more than forty years ago, I did make a bit of progress—just enough to know that, as elusive as it continues to be, enlightenment is still highly worth pursuing.

Enlightenment is a funny sort of goal, perhaps uniquely so. Full enlightenment definitely seems to be the kind of understanding that is claimed only by those who do not have it, even though they may sincerely think they do. It is quite simple, really—a kind of understanding that goes beyond "having" and "not having," claiming or not claiming. It is more like an extreme tolerance of cognitive dissonance, a complete, selfless openness that embraces both knowing and not knowing, consciousness and unconsciousness, rather than some sort of resolved state of final closure, as one might expect. That does not mean that an Enlightened One might not advance herself as competently aware in a certain context, just as she might deny any state of knowledge in another one. It is easy to forget that the "enlightened," by definition, live beyond the habitual boundaries of the alienated, self-centered person. They feel as empathetically present in others around them as they do in themselves, whereas previously all was separate and alone. So, everything the "enlightened" do or say occurs for them mostly in others' perceptions of them; their great compassion is their total openness.

"Siddhartha" is a common Indian male name; it means "one who has attained his aim." The name became famous when a prince of the Shakya nation of ancient India became the fully enlightened Buddha. His father, King Shuddhodhana, had named him Siddhartha to celebrate the auspicious circumstances of his birth and the outstanding omens of his high destiny. In choosing this name for his hero, Hesse made the Buddha a real person for his European readers by imagining what he must have gone through to become enlightened, what his enlightenment must have been like, and what this meant for any human being seeking the way and the truth.

I am impressed by Hesse's sophisticated self-restraint and intuitive respect in not attempting a dramatization of the biography of the first Siddhartha, the prince who became Shakyamuni Buddha. Instead, he created a parallel Siddhartha whose character he could freely allow to flourish in the artistic imagination. Why does Hesse tell his story in this way? Why didn't he just write a fictional account of the original Siddhartha, and tell the life of the Buddha? Did he himself disagree with the Buddha's teachings of the meaning of life and the nature of the path? How well did he know the Buddha's teachings, after all? Hesse himself says: "I am not Siddhartha, I am only always and again on my way to him."

*Siddhartha* is primarily a gripping tale, a fiction about a young man in search of the truth of life and of, most importantly, the potential to be released from inherited habits of being and achieve a higher self. Hesse's Siddhartha is a junior contemporary of the Shakya prince Siddhartha who became the Buddha. Like the prince, he grows up in privileged circumstances, with the best education available in his country and era. He has a strong spiritual opportunity as a member of the well-respected priestly and intellectual class, the Brahmins, which loosely means "the divines." (Brahma is the name of the Indian nation's personal Creator God, and *Brahman* is the Sanskrit word for "the transcendental absolute reality beyond all imagination or idea.") While still a youth, Siddhartha becomes disillusioned with his social status and priestly role and decides to join the wandering spiritual ascetics of his day. These yogis are called *shramanas*, which means "world-weary wanderers" or "seekers," those who retire from ordinary lifeways in order to seek out the higher planes of existence or even to transcend existence altogether.

Siddhartha must force his father to allow him to leave home, which is no easy task, since his leaving breaks his father's heart. But Siddhartha is determined, and eventually his father allows him to go. Taking with him his best friend, Govinda, he enters on three years of the most unimaginably tortuous ascetical disciplines. He learns extreme control of mind and body, developing near-magical powers, a great ability to concentrate, and the power to fast, wait, and think, as he himself puts it a bit later in the story. All this is a direct parallel with the life of the Siddhartha who became the Buddha. The fact that Hesse places his hero in the priestly class is significant, for it shows that Hesse knew a lot more about Vedantic Hinduism than about Buddhism. European intellectuals of the time considered the two forms of Indian thought and practice to be virtually the same.

Hesse certainly seems more familiar with the Hindu teaching of Self (the I in the current translation), or *Atman*—enlightenment as the realization of the Divine Self—rather than the Buddhist teaching of selflessness, or *anatman*. As Hesse's Siddhartha grows up a Brahmin's son, he learns the Vedic rituals and chants and is drawn to meditate on the Vedantic teachings about how to transcend the mundane little self and achieve the divine Great Self. The quest of spiritual liberation is expressed in the Upanishads, Brahminical religious texts, as the gradual discarding of all petty self-identities in order to realize the Great Self of God as one's very own deepest self. *Tat tvam asi!*, or "That Thou art!"—that is, "You are Godhead!" Or *Aham Brahma asmi!*—"I am God!": These are forms of the "great statement," or spiritual aim, of the Upanishads, and they tell the whole story.

But it is one thing to hear this or to say this, and another to experience this fully in the great release of liberation known as *moksha*. So Siddhartha becomes an adept in the yogas—methodical "yokings" or disciplines—of mind and body control, mastering the great interior technologies of India that have enabled masters to control their thoughts and inner imagery, control their breath and inner organs, die consciously and return to life at will, travel out of body, and things even more unbelievable to the modern materialist.

After many adventures, however, after mastering all that his *shramana* teachers can teach him, Siddhartha decides that the way of the ascetic also does not suffice to lead him to the higher understanding he seeks. So he again breaks with his teachers, leaves them, and decides that his path must take yet another turn. This again parallels Prince Siddhartha's decision to abandon asceticism, bathe, eat, and take his "diamond seat" at the foot of the tree of enlightenment, vowing never to break his meditation there until he should fully understand the selfless Self and all reality.

At this point our Siddhartha actually meets Gautama (family name of the Buddha), more properly known as the Shakyamuni Buddha. He and his friend Govinda spend the night in the Jetavana grove, the monastic sanctuary in which thousands of seekers are gathered around Shakyamuni, who is already widely recognized as fully enlightened. They hear the Buddha's teachings, and both accept their truth and power. Govinda is moved to abandon his ascetic's long hair and filthy rags, take refuge in the Buddha, his teachings, and his community, don the clean saffron patchwork robe, and join the order of mendicants (*bhikshu*). Siddhartha is also highly moved by the Buddha's presence, for he feels that the Buddha embodies everything he seeks, has achieved the enlightened knowledge he needs, and has realized the peace he desires. But Siddhartha has the complicating intuition that he cannot achieve what the Buddha has achieved by following the Buddha—what the Buddha has realized cannot be taught to another; each must realize it for himself. Therefore, the best way to emulate the Buddha is *not* to follow him.

Hesse says of this: "Wisdom cannot be learned. That is an experience that I had to try to represent by poetical means. The result of that attempt is *Siddhartha*." Siddhartha has a marvelous conversation with the Buddha on the topic of following a teacher as opposed to learning from one's own experience, wherein the Buddha neither approves nor disapproves of the course Siddhartha chooses, but warns him of the dangers of excessive cleverness and wishes him well along his way.

From here on, Hesse sends the story in a new direction, beyond the pattern of adventures that parallel those of Prince Siddhartha becoming the Buddha. Hesse's poetic instinct for nonduality takes him away from the pious, world-renouncing, monastic story of the Buddha, as it was understood in Europe then and still widely now; his Siddhartha returns to the world, determines that he must find enlightenment in the world—Nirvana in *samsara* (the unenlightened world of suffering)—not beyond it, not in some otherworldly, disembodied state. Hesse said of his *Siddhartha* that through the book he had "departed once and for all from the Indian way of thinking," as if through it he had exorcised the spell of India upon his mind. Ironically, by taking Siddhartha in a new direction—one he understood not to be the Buddha's—he freed himself from some sort of perceived constraint—a constraint of a religious otherworldliness, which he identified with India but which was very likely a constraint much closer to home, that of the strict Pietistic morality he had inherited from his grandfather and parents. Interestingly, some decades earlier, German philosopher Friedrich Nietzsche (1844–1900) had taken a similar turn, when, in writing *Thus Spake Zarathustra*, he dropped the Buddha as his protagonist and turned to the Persian prophet Zoroaster (or Zarathustra). Nietzsche intuitively felt that the Buddha he knew from German translations of the monastic Buddhist Pali scriptures was too "world-negating" and "otherworldly," and not strongly enough life affirming (in Indian philosophical terms, too dualistic and not nondualistic).

Hesse's grandfather had spent years in India as a missionary, and his house in Calw, near Stuttgart, where Hesse grew up, was full of

Indian artifacts, books, and artworks. Somehow India must have represented in Hesse's young mind a paradoxical blend of the exotic and spiritual with the stern Protestant morality of his grandfather and parents. Like Siddhartha, Hesse rebelled against his parents, school, and society; he endured a stormy adolescence, and was committed to a mental institution for a time when he was fifteen after he threatened to kill himself with a pistol. There were stormy times indeed in Hesse's youth, and his subsequent difficult relationships with his first wife (the mother of his three sons) and his children bore the stamp of his difficulties with his own parents and grandparents. As already mentioned, at the time he was working on *Siddhartha*, after World War I had ended, Hesse was fleeing from the catastrophe of his family situation; he left his beloved first wife in a mental institution and his children under the care of friends and relatives, and moved to southern Switzerland. The poignancy in *Siddhartha* of the youth leaving his father's house, the adept leaving the Buddha's monastic sanctuary, the lover leaving his beloved's worldly life of pleasure and artistry—these clearly resonate with Hesse's own abandonment of post–World War I Germany, his own family relationships, and his familiar setting.

Back to the story: After leaving the Buddha, Siddhartha heads toward a nearby city. There he meets his fourth great teacher, a beautiful courtesan named Kamala. From her he learns the arts of passionate love, and the two fall in love—so far as such a thing is possible for a man so consumed with transcendental things and for a woman who is an artist of the sensuous. In the process Kamala helps him find a position with a local merchant, Kamaswami (literally, "Passion-master"), and Siddhartha settles down to a life of business, pleasure, wealth, and games.

After years of this lifestyle, he loses his spiritual edge, forgets about his quest, and ends up becoming disgusted with himself. Once again he abandons all his relationships and possessions and wanders out into the forest, where he finds his fifth and sixth teachers, a wise old ferryman named Vasudeva (one of the names of the Indian god Vishnu) and the ageless, many-voiced river across which he plies his ferry. Here at the river, the story gradually draws to a close, as Siddhartha achieves a kind of surpassing peace. Hesse does not romanticize the higher life. He shows the bad with the good, unflinchingly. There are a few final bitter pills at the end of the tale. I leave you to discover them for yourself.

There's no harm in sharing the bare bones of the tale, since the world of the work is full of so much more. Hesse clearly was one of the great teachers of modern Europe. He turned away from the violence of World War I, and instead became a novelist, poet, painter, lover, and gardener. He redefined patriotism as intelligence, appreciation of nature, love of humanity with all its foibles, and peacefulness. He stood firmly against Hitler and all the insanity of World War II. He was a literary Gandhi, and the Swedish Nobel Committee was right to award him the prize for literature in 1946 for his high art as well as his message of peace. He taught Europeans that there is something better than war, to which they had been so long addicted. Today, here in America, we are no less in need of his teachings, since we seem so baffled by the European Union and its preference for peace at all costs. Can we learn the lessons of *Siddhartha*, without having to suffer such a level of violence on our own soil as the Europeans brought upon themselves twice in the last century? Eighty-five years after it was published, the message of *Siddhartha* is as fresh and relevant as ever.

At the inner level of the human heart, Siddhartha is an absorbing character. His thought is deep and subtle, and his perceptions acute and engaging. He carries us along on his great adventure. Whether or not he attains the perfect enlightenment, whether or not there is any such thing as perfect enlightenment, Siddhartha experiments with the whole range of human possibility. Gradually and yet unmistakably, he evolves as a human being to a place of peaceful universal unity as well as unwavering personal responsibility. We journey with him on a compelling pilgrimage to the deepest places in the life of the human soul. Even if we are only able to glimpse such places with our imagination while reading *Siddhartha*, it is a great first step in our own journeys—journeys we must all inevitably take.

**Robert A. F. Thurman**, a college professor and writer for more than thirty years, holds the first endowed chair in Indo-Tibetan Buddhist Studies in America, the Jey Tsong Khapa Chair at Columbia University. A recognized worldwide authority on religion and spirituality, Asian history, philosophy, and Tibetan Buddhism, he is an eloquent advocate for the relevance of Eastern ideas to our daily lives; as such, he has become a leading voice of the value of reason, peace, and compassion. He was named one of *Time* magazine's twenty-five most influential Americans and has been profiled by the *New York Times* and *People* magazine. He was the first American to be ordained as a Tibetan monk, and he has been a student and friend of His Holiness the Dalai Lama for forty years. Thurman is the cofounder and president of the nonprofit organization Tibet House New York. He is the author of numerous books, including *Inner Revolution, Essential Tibetan Buddhism,* and *Infinite Life: Seven Virtues for Living Well.*

# TRANSLATOR'S NOTE

From his home in Montagnola, Switzerland, on August 10, 1922, Hermann Hesse wrote to Romain Rolland, the French pacifist author: "I have finally finished my *Siddhartha*. It will appear in book form next winter—almost three years after I started work on it—and you shall receive a copy right away. Part One still bears a dedication to you; I have dedicated Part Two to a cousin of mine who has been living in Japan for decades, and is steeped in Eastern thought; we are especially close."[1]

Completed during the winter of 1919–1920, the first part of *Siddhartha* initially appeared in two installments in the *Neue Zürcher Zeitung* on August 6 and 7, 1920. Samuel Fischer published them together in July 1921 in his literary review *Neue Rundschau*, bearing the dedication to Rolland. There was a long hiatus between the composition of the first and second parts of *Siddhartha*. During a critical period in 1916, Hesse had put himself under the care of Dr. Josef B. Lang, one of C. G. Jung's disciples. Although Hesse and Lang remained friends until Lang's death in 1945, during this second crisis period in 1921 the author underwent analysis with Jung. Hesse got back to work on the manuscript early in 1922, and in February his cousin Wilhelm Gundert, Oriental scholar, translator, and missionary, paid him a visit. He finished the manuscript in May.

In August 1922, some months before the book *Siddhartha* came out from S. Fischer Verlag (Berlin), Hesse received an invitation from Rolland to lecture in Lugano. At the Conference of the International Women's League for Freedom and Peace, he read the ending. "[A] Hindu, or rather a Bengali, a professor of Asian history in Calcutta . . . ," Hesse wrote to his old friend Helene Welti on August 29, "afterward . . . got somebody to translate the whole thing verbatim. He turned up the following day in Montagnola, and said he was astonished and quite moved to find a European who had reached the core of Indian philosophy. . . . I very much hope that

*Siddhartha* will eventually appear in English, not for the sake of the English themselves but for those Asians and others whom it would vindicate."[2]

And it did appear, but not until twenty-nine years had passed. The first English translation of *Siddhartha* to be published was Hilda Rosner's (New Directions, 1951). What is time? In the book's ninth chapter, "The Ferryman," Siddhartha asks that man, called Vasudeva, "[H]ave you also learned this secret from the river: that time does not exist?" (p. 85).

In his introduction to this edition Robert Thurman writes of coming to *Siddhartha* at the beginning of the 1960s, setting out for India "more or less on foot" from Manhattan in 1961 to escape from "WASP-hood at Harvard. . . . Rereading *Siddhartha* now, I can clearly see its influence on my decision at twenty to leave college and the study of Western literature, philosophy, and psychology, and seek a higher enlightenment in India. . . ." (p. xvii). Toward the end of the 1960s, reading Hesse had an important influence on me as well, though it did not send me quite as far east.

For years in Brooklyn public schools I studied French. At what must have been the age of fourteen I discovered on my elder sisters' bookshelves *Demian, Siddhartha, Steppenwolf,* and *The Journey to the East.* I devoured them; I took whatever I could find by Hesse out of the library. On my own shelves now, with many other Hesse volumes, is a yellowed hardcover of *Narcissus and Goldmund* from 1968. The price is cut off the jacket flap; perhaps someone gave it to me for my fifteenth birthday.

During my last year in high school, 1969–1970, it was arranged for me to begin to study German at Brooklyn College. So my Germanic studies officially began, and later they traveled with me to New Haven (with relatively brief stops outside Salzburg, inside Vienna) and eventually from German to Swedish (with longer and repeated stops in Göteborg, Stockholm, Helsinki), and back to Brooklyn. I say "officially" because the first foreign language I was taught but can no longer read was Yiddish. It was the secret language my parents sometimes spoke with even more aged relatives, and the language we learned in the first year of an afterschool school we called cheder (Hebrew for "room") when I was eight.

*My* first book was a limited edition of Rilke translations I had done as a Yale undergraduate, published by one of the patriarchs of American fine-press printing, Harry Duncan. *Holding Out,* in his splendid Abattoir Editions, was printed on paper that was hand-made in India. My first commercial translation was a book of Hesse's poetry, *Hours in the Garden and Other Poems* (Farrar, Straus and Giroux, 1979). A few years later, I translated a selection of his tales, *Pictor's Metamorphoses and Other Fantasies* (Farrar, Straus and Giroux, 1982). But mainly it has been poetry—my own and translated from Swedish—that has consumed most of my writing time over the years. In January 2006 the inquiry came about translating *Siddhartha,* and as I arrived in class, I mentioned this to my tai chi teacher, who replied, "The Buddha smiles."

This translation is, so far as I know, the sixth of *Siddhartha* in print. Why so many? Things expire (for example, copyright terms); things change (language is one such thing); classics (even newer ones) remain classic but not constant; reading *is* interpretation.

Why read this one? Hesse considered himself first and foremost a poet.[3] Not only when he published the first part in *Neue Rundschau* but also when he published the whole book, he referred to *Siddhartha* neither as novel nor novella but as "*eine indische Dichtung,*" a work of Indic poetry. It is a prose-poem. The voice throughout is that of a storyteller—at times redundant, at times formulaic. Surely this prose-poem is meant to be heard. Again and again the value of listening is stressed.

I made the translation by listening; I read the German countless times, many of those times I read it aloud. I followed Hesse's punctuation for the sake of rhythm as far as I could, although I tried to avoid sacrificing semantics. This applies also to word order and to speech rhythm. Of course I read the English out loud many times as well. The rhythm of poetry is the rhythm of the moving body and its breath—despite his many and various health problems, Hesse walked a great deal. I hope you will read this *Siddhartha* out loud, and enjoy it!

## A few words on a few words

The absence of the word "ego" and the infrequent occurrence of the word "self" in my translation may surprise a reader who comes to this book in English alone, especially if he or she has read an earlier translation. The term that gives rise to this quandary in English is the German neuter noun "*das Ich*." In Hesse's virtually pure standard High German, "the I" is capitalized, just as all nouns were. Invariably I translate this "*Ich*" as the "I," modifying it by other parts of speech as necessary. (German personal pronouns, including "*ich*," are lowercase.) Where Hesse actually uses the noun "*Selbst*" (also neuter), or the pronoun "*selbst*," I give the word "self." I have long suspected we all may have been better off if Freud's "*das Ich*" had never been rendered as the Latinate "ego."

Not only from biographical data and Hesse's voluminous correspondence but also from his autobiographical writings, essays, and book reviews,[4] we know that Hesse read and appreciated both Freud and Jung. For Jung, "ego" and "self" were quite different terms. In *Siddhartha*, "*Ich*" and "*Selbst*" appear at times to be synonymous, at other times distinct, as you will see.

Hesse's sole physical journey to the East took place in 1911, and despite his intention to visit the Malabar Coast, where his parents and grandparents had done missionary work, he did not set foot on the Indian subcontinent. He visited *Indien*, the Indies, the East Indies—Penang, Singapore, Sumatra, Ceylon (Sri Lanka), Borneo, Burma (Myanmar). *The Journey to the East* came out in 1932; its German title, *Die Morgenlandfahrt*, also suggests the Crusades. There are many good reasons to allow all the tones of "*das Ich*" to resonate as widely and openly as possible on our author's psycho-spiritual journey, one that continues as we go on reading his various works in various languages over time.

All his life Hesse read extensively in things Eastern: the Vedas and Upanishads, Buddhist texts (among them his cousin Wilhelm Gundert's 1912 translation of the *Bi Yän Lu*), the *Tao Te Ching*, and much else. In his autobiographical sketch from 1923, "Childhood of the Magician," he pays tribute to his mother's father, Dr. Hermann Gundert (1814–1893), a Swabian Pietist who spoke many Indian languages and authored a Malayalam grammar and a Malayalam-English dictionary. It is difficult to say from which original languages the German—and likely additional—translations Hesse read came. For the present translation, I have relied on Prof. Robert Thurman for guidance with the transcription of historical Indian names and terms. I trust these will be familiar to contemporary American readers.

RIKA LESSER
*(March 2007)*

---

**Rika Lesser** is the author of three books of poetry: *Etruscan Things*, *All We Need of Hell*, and *Growing Back*, and the forthcoming *Questions of Love*. She has published five books of poetry in translation—by Claes Andersson, Gunnar Ekelöf, Hermann Hesse, Rainer Maria Rilke, and Göran Sonnevi—as well as translations of various works of Swedish and German fiction for adults and young people. She has received many grants and awards for her work, among them the Academy of American Poets Landon Translation Prize, the Poetry Translation Prize of the Swedish Academy, fellowships from the Fulbright Commission and the National Endowment for the Arts, and twice the American-Scandinavian Foundation Translation Prize. She co-chaired the PEN Translation Committee from 1989 to 1995 and has taught poetry or literary translation at Columbia, the George Washington University, the New School, Yale, and the 92nd Street Y in New York City. Rika Lesser lives in Brooklyn Heights, New York.

### Notes

1. Quoted in *Soul of the Age: Selected Letters of Hermann Hesse, 1891–1962*, edited with an introduction by Theodore Ziolkowski, translated by Mark Harman (New York: Farrar, Straus and Giroux, 1991), p. 117.
2. Ibid., p. 118.
3. Besides *Hours in the Garden*, there have also been available in English for some time *Poems* (New York: Farrar, Straus and Giroux, 1970), selected and translated by James Wright, all on the theme of homesickness; and

*Crisis: Pages from a Diary* (New York: Farrar, Straus and Giroux, 1975), translated by Ralph Manheim—the poems Hesse had to be persuaded to publish separately from *Steppenwolf*.

4. See, for example, Ralph Freedman's *Hermann Hesse: Pilgrim of Crisis* (New York: Pantheon Books, 1978); and Hermann Hesse's *Autobiographical Writings* (New York: Farrar, Straus and Giroux, 1972) and *My Belief: Essays on Life and Art* (New York: Farrar, Straus and Giroux, 1974).

# SIDDHARTHA

*Part One*

TO ROMAIN ROLLAND
REVERED FRIEND

# THE SON OF THE BRAHMIN

In the shade of the house, in the sunlight on the riverbank near the boats, in the shade of the sal tree forest, in the shade of the banyan fig Siddhartha[1] grew up, the handsome son of the Brahmin,[2] the young falcon, together with Govinda, his friend,[3] the son of a Brahmin. Sunshine browned his pale shoulders on the riverbank, while bathing, during the ritual ablutions, during the sacred offerings. Shadows flowed into his dark eyes in the mango grove, when at play with other boys, while his mother sang, while the sacred offerings were made, while his father the scholar gave instruction, while the wise men conversed. Siddhartha had already been participating for quite some time in the discussions of the sages, with Govinda he practiced debating, with Govinda he practiced the art of concentration, in the service of meditative absorption. Already he understood how to speak the Om[4] without a sound, the word of words, soundlessly pronouncing it within while inhaling, soundlessly speaking it out while exhaling, his soul gathered in, composed, his brow surrounded by radiance, ringed with the glow of his clear-thinking mind. Already he understood, within the interior of his being he recognized Atman, indestructible, at one with the universe.

His father's heart skipped joyously for this son who was quick to learn, who was thirsty for knowledge; in him he saw growing a great sage and priest, a prince among the Brahmins.

Rapture made his mother's breast flutter—whenever she saw him, when she saw him stride along, when she saw him sit down or stand up, Siddhartha, the strong one, the handsome one, he who strode on slender legs, he who greeted her with perfect decorum.

Love stirred in the hearts of the young daughters of Brahmins when Siddhartha walked down the city's alleyways, with his radiant brow, with the eye of a king, with his narrow hips.

More than all of them, though, his friend Govinda, the son of a Brahmin, loved him. He loved Siddhartha's eyes and gracious voice, he loved his gait and the perfect decorum of all his movements, he loved everything Siddhartha did and said, and most of all he loved his mind, his lofty, impassioned thinking, his fervent purpose, his high calling. Govinda knew: this would be no ordinary Brahmin, no idle sacrificial official, no greedy merchant of magic formulae, no vain empty orator, no mean conniving priest, neither would he be a silly simple sheep in the herd of the many. No, nor did he, Govinda, want to be one among ten thousand Brahmins. He wanted to follow his beloved, his magnificent Siddhartha. And if ever Siddhartha were to become a god, if he were to arrive among the radiant,[5] then Govinda wanted to follow him, as his friend, his companion, as his servant, his spearman, his shadow.

Everyone loved Siddhartha in this way. He brought delight to everyone; to everyone he was a pleasure.

But he, Siddhartha, did not delight himself, he was no pleasure to himself. Ambling down the rosy paths of the fig garden, sitting in the bluish shade of the meditation grove, washing his limbs daily in the expiatory bath, making sacrifices in the deep shade of the mango forest, with perfect decorum in all his gestures, beloved by all, a joy to all, in his own heart he still bore no joy. Dreams came to him and turbulent thoughts came flowing from the river water, sparkling from the night stars, melting from the sun's rays; dreams came to him and a restlessness of his soul rose in the smoke from the sacrifices, breathed from the verses of the Rig Veda,[6] trickled down from the teachings of the old Brahmins.

Within himself Siddhartha had begun to nourish discontent. He had begun to feel that the love of his father and the love of his mother and even the love of his friend Govinda would not forever after delight him, soothe him, satisfy and suffice him. He had begun to surmise that his venerable father and his other teachers, that these wise Brahmins had already conveyed the majority and the best part of their wisdom, that they had already poured out their plenty into his waiting vessel, and the vessel was not full, the mind was not satisfied, the soul was not calm, the heart not stilled. Ablutions were good, but they were water, they did not wash away sin, they did not quench spiritual thirst, they did not dissolve fear in the heart. Sacrificing to the gods and invoking them was excellent—but was this all? Did sacrifices bring happiness? And what was the nature of the gods?[7] Was it really Prajapati who had created the world? Was it not the Atman, He, the Sole One, the All-One? Were not the gods representations, created as you and I, subject to time, transitory? Was it therefore good, was it right, was it a meaningful and supreme act to sacrifice to the gods? To whom else was one to sacrifice, whom else was one to venerate, besides Him, the Only One, the Atman? And where was Atman to be found, where did He abide, where did His eternal heart beat, where else but within one's own I, deep inside, in what is indestructible, borne within every individual? But where, where was this innermost and ultimate I? The great sages taught that it was not flesh and bone, it was neither thought nor consciousness. Where, where then was it to be found? To press toward there, to penetrate to the I, to me, to the Atman—was there another path worth seeking? Alas, no one showed the way, no one knew it, not one's father, not the teachers or the sages, not the holy sacrificial hymns! The Brahmins and their sacred books knew everything, everything! They had seen to everything and more: the creation of the world, the origin of speech, of food, of inhalation, of exhalation, the order of the senses, the deeds of the gods—they knew infinitely much—but was there value in knowing everything if one did not know the one and only thing, the single most important thing, the only thing that matters?

Certainly, many verses of the holy books, splendid verses, especially in the Upanishads of the Sama Veda,[8] spoke of this, the innermost and ultimate. "Your soul is the entire world," so it is written there, and it is also written that when a person is asleep, in deep sleep, he enters into his innermost place and abides in Atman. Wondrous wisdom exists in these verses, all that the sages know is gathered here in magical words, pure as honey gathered by bees. No, this enormous quantity of knowledge, gathered and preserved here by countless generations of wise Brahmins was not to be despised. —But where were the Brahmins, where the priests, the sages or penitents who had succeeded in having this the deepest knowledge not only in their minds but also in their experience? Where was the initiate who could magically conjure intimacy with Atman from deep sleep into waking life, into every move, into every word and deed?[9] Siddhartha knew many venerable Brahmins, his father best of all, the pure one, the scholar most highly revered. His father was admirable, his conduct calm and noble, his life pure, his words wise; fine, noble thoughts occupied his brow—but he, too, like so many who had acquired knowledge, did he live in bliss, was he at peace, was he not still a seeker, did he not thirst? Did he not return again and again, thirsting, to the holy sources, to drink, to sacrifice, to read the books, to engage in dialogue with other Brahmins? Why must he, who was blameless, wash sin away daily, take pains to purify himself every day, day after day after day? Did not Atman dwell inside him, did not the primal source flow within his own heart? It had to be found, the primal source within the individual I, one had to possess it oneself! Everything else was searching, sidestepping, going astray.

Such was Siddhartha's thinking, such was his thirst, such his suffering.

Often he would say these words from a section of the Chandogya Upanishad[10] to himself: "Yea, of this Brahman the name is Satyam—the True; he who knows this enters every day into heaven."[11] Often it seemed near, the heavenly world, but he had never quite reached it, never extinguished the ultimate thirst. And among all the wise and most sagacious men he knew and whose instruction he savored, among them all there was not one who had quite reached heaven, who had entirely quenched his eternal thirst.

"Govinda," Siddhartha said to his friend, "dear Govinda, let us walk to the banyan tree, it is time for us to practice our meditation."

They walked to the banyan tree, they sat down, here Siddhartha, twenty paces farther Govinda. As he sat down, ready to speak the Om, in a murmur Siddhartha repeated this verse:

> Om is the bow, soul is the arrow,
> Brahman is the arrow's goal,
> One must strike it undiverted.

When the usual period for the meditation exercise was over, Govinda rose. Evening had come, it was time to perform the evening ablution. He called Siddhartha's name. Siddhartha gave no answer. Siddhartha was sitting totally immersed, his eyes rigidly fixed and focused on a very distant goal, the tip of his tongue protruded slightly between his teeth; he seemed not to be breathing. That is how he sat, cocooned in contemplation. Thinking Om, his soul dispatched as an arrow toward Brahman.[12]

AT ONE TIME shramanas[13] had passed through Siddhartha's city, ascetics on a pilgrimage, three scrawny, faded men, neither old nor young, dust and blood on their shoulders, nearly naked, scorched by the sun, ringed by solitude, alien and hostile to the world, foreigners and haggard jackals in the realm of human beings. Behind them a breeze blew hot with the scent of silent passion, of mortification, of ruthless self-denial.

In the evening, after the time for meditation, Siddhartha spoke to Govinda, saying: "Tomorrow morning, my friend, Siddhartha will go to the shramanas. He will become a shramana."[14]

Govinda blanched when he heard the words and read in his friend's impassive face a decision from which he would not swerve, like the arrow flying fast from the bow. In that very moment and at first sight Govinda knew: Now it is beginning, now Siddhartha is going his own way, now a seed has been planted, as his fate sprouts, so does mine. And he went pale as a dry banana peel.

"O Siddhartha," he cried, "will your father permit it?"

Siddhartha looked across at him like one who had been awakened. Quick as an arrow he read Govinda's soul, read the fear, read the devotion.

"O Govinda," he spoke gently, "let us not waste words. Tomorrow at daybreak I will begin the life of the shramanas. Speak no more of it."

Siddhartha walked into the room where his father sat on a mat made of bast; he walked behind his father and stood there until his father sensed someone standing behind him. The Brahmin spoke: "Is it you, Siddhartha? Tell me then what you have come here to say."[15]

Siddhartha spoke: "With your permission, Father. I have come to tell you that I wish tomorrow to depart your house and go to the ascetics. It is my wish to become a shramana. May it please my father not to oppose this."

The Brahmin held silence, was silent so long that in the small window the stars shifted and changed their pattern before the silence in the room came to an end. Mute and motionless the son stood with his arms folded in front of him; mute and motionless the father sat on the mat, and the stars traveled across the sky. Then the father spoke: "It is unbecoming for a Brahmin to speak vehement or angry words. But my heart is vexed. I would not like to hear this request from your lips a second time."

Slowly the Brahmin rose, Siddhartha stood mute, his arms folded.

"What are you waiting for?" his father asked.

Siddhartha spoke: "You know that."

Displeased his father left the room, displeased he sought his bed and lay down.

After one hour, when no sleep came to his eyes, the Brahmin stood up, paced back and forth, stepped outside the house. Through the small window he looked into the room, there he saw Siddhartha standing, arms folded, undisturbed. His bright overgarment had a pale sheen. Vexed at heart, his father turned and went back to his bed.

After one hour, when no sleep came to his eyes, the Brahmin stood up again, paced back and forth, stepped outside the house, beheld the risen moon. Through the window he looked into the room, there stood Siddhartha, undisturbed, arms folded, moonlight gleamed on his bare shins. Uneasy at heart, the father took to his bed.

And he returned after one hour, and returned again after two hours, looked through the little window, saw Siddhartha standing in the light of the moon, of the stars, in the darkness. And returned hour after hour, held his silence, looked into the room, saw the figure standing there undisturbed, filled his heart with anger, filled his heart with worry, filled his heart with trepidation, filled it with woe.

And in the last hour of the night, before daybreak, he turned back, came into the room, beheld the standing youth who looked large and foreign to him.

"Siddhartha," he said, "what are you waiting for?"

"You know that."

"Will you stand and wait like that forever, until it is day, and noon, and evening?"

"I will stand and wait."

"You will grow tired, Siddhartha."

"I will grow tired."

"You will fall asleep, Siddhartha."

"I will not fall sleep."

"You will die, Siddhartha."

"I will die."

"And you would rather die than obey your father?"

"Siddhartha has always obeyed his father."

"So you mean to abandon your plan?"

"Siddhartha will do what his father tells him."

The first light of day fell into the chamber. The Brahmin saw that Siddhartha's knees were trembling slightly. He saw no sign of trembling in Siddhartha's face, the eyes looked off into the distance. Then the father acknowledged that Siddhartha was no longer with him and in his home, that now he had already left him.

His father touched Siddhartha's shoulder.

"You will," he spoke, "go into the forest and be a shramana. Having found bliss in the forest, come and teach me bliss. If you find disappointment, then come back and together again let us sacrifice to the gods. Go now and kiss your mother, tell her where you are going. For me, though, it is time to go to the river and perform the first ablution."

He took his hand from his son's shoulder and went outside. Siddhartha reeled to one side when he tried to walk. He mastered his legs, bowed before his father and went to his mother to do as his father bade him.

When in the first light of day, stiff-legged, he slowly left the still silent city, near the last hut a cowering shadow rose up and attached itself to the pilgrim—Govinda.

"You have come," Siddhartha said and smiled.

"I have come," said Govinda.

# WITH THE SHRAMANAS

On the evening of this day they caught up with the ascetics, the sere shramanas, and offered them companionship and obedience. They were accepted.

Siddhartha gave his robe to a poor Brahmin on the street. Now he wore only a loincloth and an unstitched shawl, the color of earth. He ate but once a day, and never any cooked food. He fasted for fifteen days. He fasted for twenty-eight days. The flesh melted from his thighs and cheeks. Hot dreams flickered from his enlarged eyes; on his withering fingers the nails grew long and on his chin a dry, bristly beard. His gaze turned to ice when he encountered women; his mouth winced with scorn when he walked through a city where people dressed in their finery. He saw merchants doing business, princes going hunting, mourners bewailing their dead, whores offering themselves, physicians caring for the sick, priests determining the day for sowing, lovers loving, mothers quieting their children—and none of this merited a single glance of his eye, it was all a lie, it all stank, it all stank of lies, it all feigned significance, good fortune and beauty, and it was all unavowed putrefaction. The taste of the world was bitter. Life was affliction.[16]

Siddhartha had a single goal before him, one and one only: to become empty, empty of thirst, empty of desire, empty of dreams, empty of joy and pain. To die away from himself, no longer to be I, to find the peace of the emptied heart, by thinking away from the self to stand open to the miraculous: this was his goal. When the entire I was conquered and dead, when every passion, every drive in the heart was still, then the ultimate had to awaken, what was innermost, most essential in being, that which is no longer I, the great secret.

Keeping silence Siddhartha stood in the vertical blaze of the sun, glowing with pain, glowing with thirst, and stood until he no longer felt any pain or thirst. Silent he stood in the rainy season, water ran down from his hair over his freezing shoulders, over his freezing hips and legs, and the penitent stood until his shoulders and legs no longer froze, until they were silent, until they were still. Keeping silence he squatted among bramblebushes, from his burning skin oozed blood, from the abscesses pus, and Siddhartha remained rigid, remained motionless until the blood ceased flowing, until the stinging came to nothing, until the burning came to nothing.

Siddhartha sat erect and learned to slow his breathing, learned how to manage with little breath, learned how to stop breathing. He learned, beginning with the breath, to lower his pulse, learned to slow the beating of his heart until it was so diminished that it scarcely existed.

Instructed by the eldest of the shramanas, Siddhartha practiced moving away from the self, practiced meditation, following new rules, the shramanas' rules. A heron flew over the bamboo forest— and Siddhartha took the heron into his soul, flew over the forest and the mountains, was the heron, gobbled fish, hungered as a heron hungers, spoke heron croak, died the death of a heron. A dead jackal lay on the sandy shore, and Siddhartha's soul slid inside its corpse, became the dead jackal, lay on the strand, swelled up, stank, putrefied, was dismembered by hyenas, skinned by vultures, became bones, dust, blew in open country. And Siddhartha's soul returned, died, decayed, turned to dust, tasted the muddy rush of the cycle, waiting in new thirst like a hunter for the gap where the cycle could be escaped, where the end of causes, where eternity free of suffering would begin. He mortified his senses, he slew his memory, he slid out of his I into a thousand alien shapes, became beast, carrion, stone, wood, water, and found himself every time awakening again, in the light of the sun or the moon, again he was I, whirling around in the round, he felt thirst, conquered thirst, felt thirst anew.

Siddhartha learned a great deal among the shramanas, he learned to walk many paths away from the I. He walked the path of self-distancing through pain, through voluntary endurance of suffering and vanquishing of pain, of hunger, of thirst, of exhaustion. He walked the path of self-distancing through meditation, by emptying the mind of all associations. He learned to walk these and other paths, thousands of times he abandoned his I, for hours and days he abided in the not-I. But wheresoever the paths might lead away from the I, their end always led back to the I. If Siddhartha fled the I a thousand times—remaining in nothingness, in animals, in stones—his return was unavoidable, inescapable the hour when again he found himself in sunlight or moonlight, in shadow or in rain, and again was I, again Siddhartha, and again experienced the torment of the obligatory cycle.

By his side lived Govinda, his shadow, walking the same path, submitting himself to the same exertions. They seldom spoke to each other except as their duty and exercises required. At times they went through the villages two by two, begging for sustenance for themselves and their teachers.

"What do you think, Govinda," Siddhartha said one day while they made their rounds begging. "What do you think, have we come any further? Have we reached any goals?"

Govinda replied: "We have learned, and we will go on learning. You will be a great shramana, Siddhartha. You have learned every exercise quickly; the old shramanas have often marveled at you. One day you will become a saint, o Siddhartha."

Siddhartha spoke: "It does not seem that way to me, my friend. What I have learned up to this day with the shramanas, this, o Govinda, I could have learned more quickly and more simply: In any tavern in a brothel district, my friend, among men who haul freight and play at dice I could have learned it."

Govinda spoke: "Siddhartha is joking with me. How could you have learned meditation, how could you have learned to hold your breath, how could you have learned indifference to hunger and pain there among those poor wretches?"

And Siddhartha said softly, as if speaking to himself: "What is meditation? What is departure from the body? What is fasting? What is holding the breath? It is flight from the I, it is a brief escape from the torment of being an I, it is a brief anodyne against the pain and the senselessness of life. The drover of oxen finds the same escape, the same numbing stupor at the inn when he drinks a few bowls of rice wine or fermented coconut milk. Then he ceases to be conscious of his self, he no longer feels the pangs of life, he is briefly anesthetized. Asleep over his bowl of rice wine, he finds the same thing that Siddhartha and Govinda find when in their long exercises they seep out of their bodies, escaping, lingering in the not-I.[17] That is how it is, o Govinda."

Govinda spoke: "So you say, o Friend, and yet you know that Siddhartha is no drover of oxen and a shramana is no drunkard. The drinker may well numb himself, he may briefly flee and rest, but he returns from his delirium and finds everything just as it was of old, is none the wiser for it, has gained no knowledge, has not risen to a higher level."

And Siddhartha spoke with a smile, "This I do not know, I have never been a drinker. But that I, Siddhartha, find only brief anodyne in my exercises and meditations and am just as far from wisdom and release as a child in his mother's womb, this, o Govinda, this I know."

And again for a second time, when Siddhartha left the woods with Govinda to go begging for sustenance for their brothers and teachers, Siddhartha began to speak and said: "Do you think, o Govinda, we are on the right path now? Are we actually approaching knowledge? Are we actually approaching deliverance? Or are we not perhaps going in a circle—we who were contemplating escaping the cycle."

Govinda spoke: "We have learned much, Siddhartha, there is still much to learn. We are not going in a circle, we are going upward, the circle is a spiral, we have already ascended many steps."

Siddhartha answered: "How old, do you think, is our eldest shramana, our most venerable teacher?"

Govinda replied: "Our eldest has reached perhaps the age of sixty years."

And Siddhartha: "Sixty years old, and he has not attained nirvana.[18] He will be seventy and eighty, and you and I, we will grow just as old and we will practice, and we will fast, and we will meditate. But we will not attain nirvana, neither he nor we. O Govinda, I believe that among all the shramanas that exist maybe not one, not a single one will attain nirvana. We find consolations, we find anodynes, we learn technical skills with which we deceive ourselves. But we do not find the essential, the path of paths."

"Would you please, nonetheless," Govinda spoke up, "not pronounce such terrifying words, Siddhartha! How could it be possible then, among so many learned men, among so many Brahmins, among so many austere and venerable shramanas, among so many seeking, so many inwardly devoted, so many holy men, that no one should find the way of ways?"

Siddhartha however answered in a voice, containing as much sadness as scorn, in a gentle voice, somewhat sorry, somewhat mocking: "Soon, Govinda, your friend will abandon the footpath of the shramanas, which he has walked with you for such a long time. I thirst, o Govinda, and on this long shramana pathway my thirst has in no way diminished. I have always thirsted for knowledge, I have always been full of questions. Year after year I have asked the Brahmins, and year after year I have asked the holy Vedas, and year after year I have asked the pious shramanas. Maybe, o Govinda, it would have been just as well, it would have been just as wise and equally beneficial if I had asked the hornbill or the chimpanzee. I have spent a long time and I have still not finished learning, o Govinda, that one can learn nothing! In actuality, so I believe, there is no such *thing* we call by the name of 'learning.' There is, o my friend, only one knowledge, this is everywhere, this is Atman, in me and in you and in every single creature.[19] And so I am starting to believe: this knowledge has no worse enemy than the desire to know, than learning."

Then Govinda stopped still on the road, raised his hands and declared: "Please, Siddhartha, would you please refrain from alarming your friend with such talk! Truly, your words awake fear in my heart. And just think: what of the sanctity of prayer, what of the venerable caste of Brahmins, what of the holiness of the shramanas, if what you say were so, if there were no learning?! What, o Siddhartha, what then would become of it all, what on earth is holy, has value, is venerable?!"

And Govinda murmured a verse to himself, a verse from one of the Upanishads:

> Whosoever in contemplation, pure in spirit,
>> immerses himself in Atman,
> Inexpressible in words is his heart's bliss.

But Siddhartha held his silence. He considered the words Govinda had spoken to him and thought them out to their conclusion.

Yes, he thought, standing with his head still lowered, what will remain of all this that seemed sacred to us? What remains? What stands the test of time? And he shook his head.

One day, when the two youths had been living with the shramanas for about three years' time and had participated in their devotions, by various ways and byways a piece of news, a rumor, a tale reached them: Someone had appeared, someone named Gautama, the Exalted One, the Buddha,[20] who within himself had overcome the suffering of the world and brought the wheel of rebirth to a standstill.[21] Teaching, surrounded by disciples, he traveled through the land, with no possessions, no home, no wife, in the yellow cloak of an ascetic, but with a serene brow, one of the blessed, and Brahmins and princes bowed down before him and became his pupils.

This story, this rumor, this tale resounded, rose like a fragrant aroma, here and there, in the cities the Brahmins spoke of it, in the forest the shramanas, again and again the name of Gautama, of the Buddha, entered the ears of the youths, for good and for ill, it was praised and defamed.

As when plague rules throughout a land, and word comes and begins to circulate that there is a man, a wise man, a knowledgeable man whose words and aura suffice to heal everyone stricken by the scourge, and as when these tidings spread through the land, and then everyone speaks of it, many believe, many doubt, but many just as soon take to the road to seek out the wise man, the helper, that is how this legend spread through the land, this fragrant tale of Gautama, the Buddha, the wise man from the Shakya clan. Those who believed in him spoke of his possessing the highest knowledge, he remembered his former lives, he had attained nirvana and never more returned to the cycle of rebirth, never again immersing himself in the muddy river of forms. Much that was splendid and incredible would be told of him, he had worked miracles, conquered the devil, conversed with the gods. But his enemies and those who were nonbelievers said, this Gautama is an idle tempter, he wastes his days in profligacy, he despises the sacrifices, is without erudition, knowing neither practice nor castigation.[22]

Sweet sounded the tale of Buddha, the scent of magic wafted from these reports. Yes, the world was sick, life was difficult to endure—and look, here a wellspring seemed to burst forth, here the call of a messenger seemed to sound, consoling, tender, full of noble promises. Everywhere, wherever rumor of the Buddha spread, through every region of India, youths pricked up their ears, felt longing, felt hope, and among the sons of Brahmins in the cities and villages every pilgrim and stranger was welcome, if he brought word of him, the Exalted One, the Shakyamuni.

Even to the shramanas in the forest, even to Siddhartha, even to Govinda the legend had come, slowly, drop by drop, every drop heavy with hope, every drop heavy with doubt. They spoke little of it, for the eldest shramana was no friend of this story. He had heard that this alleged Buddha previously had been an ascetic and lived in the forest, but that he had then returned to a life of luxury and worldly pleasures; he had no respect for this Gautama.[23]

"O Siddhartha," Govinda said one day to his friend. "Today I was in the village, and a Brahmin invited me into his house, and inside his house was a Brahmin's son from Magadha, who had seen the Buddha with his own eyes and had heard him teaching. How truly painful then was the breath in my bosom, and to myself I thought: If only I too, if only the two of us, Siddhartha and I, might live to experience, to hear the teachings from the lips of that Perfect One! Speak, Friend, do we not also want to go there and hear the teachings from the lips of the Buddha?"

Siddhartha spoke: "O Govinda, I had always thought Govinda would remain with the shramanas, I had always believed his goal would be to reach the age of sixty or seventy years, always continuing to practice the arts and exercises that are the adornment of the shramanas. But lo, how little did I know Govinda, too little did I know his heart. So now, dearest one, you wish to strike a new path and to follow it, where the Buddha proclaims his teachings."

Govinda spoke: "You take pleasure in being scornful. Scorn me if you like, Siddhartha! But has there not also awakened in you a longing, a desire to hear these teachings? Did you not tell me once, that you would not be following the path of the shramanas much longer?"

Then Siddhartha laughed, in his way, the tone of his voice took on a shading of sorrow and a shade of scorn, and he said: "Yes, Govinda, you have spoken well, you have remembered correctly. Please be so kind also to remember what else you heard me say, namely that I have become suspicious and tired of instruction and learning, and that I have little faith in words that have come to us from our teachers. Now then, my dear, I am prepared to hear that teaching—even if in my heart I believe that we have already sampled the finest fruit of that instruction."

Govinda spoke: "Your readiness gladdens my heart. But tell me, how should this be possible? How should the teachings of the Gautama, even before we have heard them, already have disclosed to us the best of the harvest?"

Siddhartha replied: "Let us enjoy this fruit and await what is to come, o Govinda! But the fruit we even now owe to the Gautama consists in his having called us away from the shramanas. If he has something still more and better to give us, o Friend, let us await that with our hearts at peace."

On this same day Siddhartha let the eldest of the shramanas know of his decision, that he wanted to leave. He informed the eldest with all the politeness and deference befitting a disciple and pupil. The shramana, however, upon learning that the two young men would abandon him, flew into a rage, and he ranted and raved and reviled them.

Govinda was frightened and discomfited, but Siddhartha lowered his lips and whispered into Govinda's ear: "Now I will show the old man that I have learned something from him."

With that he drew close to the shramana and stood before him, having gathered in his soul, he caught the gaze of the old man with his own, captivated him, made him mute, made him lose his will, subjected him to his own, commanding him to do, without a sound, whatever was demanded of him. The old man grew mute, his eyes were transfixed, his will was paralyzed, his arms hung limp, Siddhartha's enchantment left him utterly powerless. But Siddhartha's thoughts took possession of the shramana, he had to discharge what they ordered him to do. And so the old man bowed down several times, performed consecrating gestures, stammered out a pious farewell wish. And with thanks the youths reciprocated the bows, returned the wish, departing the place amidst these formalities.[24]

On the road Govinda said: "O Siddhartha, you learned more from the shramanas than I knew. It is difficult, it is very difficult, to bewitch an old shramana. Truly, if you had remained there, you would soon have learned how to walk on water."

"I do not wish to know how to walk on water," Siddhartha said. "May old shramanas content themselves with such wiles!"

# GAUTAMA

In the city of Savatthi, every child knew the name of the Exalted Buddha, and every house was prepared to extend charity to Gautama's disciples, to fill the bowls of the silent petitioners. Close by the city lay Gautama's favorite abode, the Jetavana, a grove given to him and his followers as a gift by the wealthy merchant Anathapindika, a humble and devoted admirer of the Exalted One.

It was toward this precinct that all the stories pointed, as did all the answers the two young ascetics received while searching for Gautama's residence. And when they arrived in Savatthi, scarcely had they come to the first house, before whose door they stood begging for food, than they were offered food, and accepted it, and Siddhartha asked the woman who gave the food to them:

"Please, most generous hostess, we would so much like to know where the Buddha, the most Venerable One, abides, for we are two shramanas from the forest, and we have come to see him, the Perfect One, and to hear him teach his teachings, to hear them from his own lips."

The woman answered: "You have truly come to the right place, you shramanas from the forest. For in Jetavana, in Anathapindika's garden, there does the Exalted One reside. There, pilgrims, you may spend the night, for in that place there is room enough for the multitudes who come streaming to hearken to the teachings as they issue from his lips."

Govinda was delighted, and filled with joy he cried out: "Well then, we have reached our goal and our road is at an end! But tell us, mother of all pilgrims, do you know him, the Buddha, have you seen him with your own eyes?"

The woman spoke: "Many times have I seen him, the Exalted One. On many days I have seen him walk through the alleyways, keeping silence, in his yellow cloak, how in silence he extends his beggar's bowl at the doors of the houses, how he walks away carrying a full bowl."

Enchanted, Govinda listened, wanting to ask more questions and to hear more. But Siddhartha admonished them to go on. They said their thanks and left and hardly needed to ask as they went along, for quite a few pilgrims and monks from Gautama's community were on their way to the Jetavana. And when they reached it in the night, there, in that very place was a continual reception, constant outcry and discussion of the needs and requirements for lodging. The two shramanas who had been living in the woods quickly and noiselessly found shelter and took their rest until morning.

When the sun rose they saw with astonishment what a huge band of the faithful and the curious had spent the night here. On all the paths of the lovely grove monks in yellow robes were wandering; here and there they sat under the trees, lost in meditation or in spiritual conversation; the shady gardens were like a city to behold, full of people swarming like bees. The majority of monks went out into the city with their bowls to collect food for the midday meal, the only one of the day. Even the Buddha himself, the Enlightened One, was in the habit of making the beggar's rounds in the morning.

Siddhartha saw him, and recognized him immediately, as if a god had pointed the man out to him.[25] He saw a modest man in a yellow cowl, carrying a beggar's bowl in his hand, walking calmly away.

"Look!" he said softly to Govinda. "That man is the Buddha."

Attentively Govinda turned his gaze toward the monk in the yellow cowl, who in no way appeared any different from the hundreds of other monks. And soon Govinda also recognized it: This is the man. And they followed after him and carefully observed him.

The Buddha went his way, unassuming and sunk in contemplation, his still countenance was neither happy nor sad, it seemed gently to smile inwardly. With a hidden smile, calm, peaceful, not unlike a healthy child, the Buddha walked, wearing the robe and setting his foot just as all his monks did, exactly as prescribed. But his face and his tread, his calmly lowered gaze, his calmly hanging hand, and from that calmly downward-hanging hand every single finger expressed peace, expressed perfection, sought nothing, imitated nothing, breathed softly in an everlasting repose, an unfading light, an inviolable peace.[26]

And so Gautama wandered on toward the city to collect alms, and the two shramanas recognized him solely by the perfection of his composure, by the stillness of his figure, in which no seeking, no wanting, no imitation, no exertion was to be discerned, only light and peace.

"Today we shall hearken to the teachings from his own lips. Today we shall hear his very words," said Govinda.

Siddhartha gave no answer. He was less curious about the teachings, he did not believe that they would teach him anything new, although he had, just like Govinda, again and again heard the content of the teachings of the Buddha, even if only from second- and third-hand reports. But he gazed attentively at Gautama's head, at his shoulders, at his feet, at his hand that hung calmly, and it seemed to him that every joint of every finger of this hand was a teaching that spoke, breathed, smelled of, glistened with truth. This man, this Buddha, was true even down to the gesture of his little finger.[27] This man was holy. Never had Siddhartha so venerated a human being, never had he so loved a human being as he did this one.

The two of them followed the Buddha to the edge of the city and silently turned around, for they themselves thought to abstain from eating on this day. They saw Gautama return, saw him partake of the meal within the circle of his disciples—what he ate could not have satisfied a bird—and saw him draw back into the shade of the mango trees.

But in the evening, as the heat subsided and everything in the camp came to life and everyone gathered, they heard the Buddha preach. They heard his voice, and it too was perfect, it was of perfect calm, it was full of peace. Gautama taught the lesson of suffering, of the origin of suffering, of the way to abrogate suffering. His quiet speech flowed calm and clear. Life was suffering, the world was full of suffering, but release from suffering had been found: Whoever followed the path of the Buddha found release.[28] With a firm yet gentle voice the Exalted One spoke, taught the four principles, taught the eightfold path, patiently he walked the accustomed path of the teachings, of examples, of repetitions, lucid and quiet his voice hovered above the listeners, like a light, like a starry sky.

When the Buddha—night had already come—finished his speech, many a pilgrim came forward and asked to be received into the community, taking refuge in the teachings. And Gautama accepted them, by saying: "You have heard the teachings well, they have been preached well. Come to us and walk in blessedness, prepare an end to all suffering."

Behold, then Govinda also stepped forward, the shy one, and spoke, "I too appeal to the Exalted One and to his teaching," and asked for acceptance among the disciples, and was accepted.

Immediately afterward, when the Buddha himself had retired for his night's rest, Govinda turned to Siddhartha and spoke eagerly: "Siddhartha, it is not my place to reproach you. Both of us have listened to the Exalted One, both of us have understood the teachings. Govinda has heard the sermon, he has taken his refuge in it. But you, my esteemed one, do you not also want to walk the path of deliverance? Do you want to hesitate, do you still want to wait?"

Siddhartha awakened as out of sleep, when he understood Govinda's words. For a long time he gazed into Govinda's face. Then he spoke gently in a voice without a trace of scorn: "Govinda, my friend, now you have taken the step, now you have chosen the path. Always, o Govinda, you have been my friend, always you have walked one step behind me. Often I have thought: Will Govinda never once take a step alone, without me, from his own soul? See, now you have become a man and you yourself are choosing your path. May you walk it to the end, o my friend. May you find release!"

Govinda, who did not yet completely understand, repeated his question in an impatient tone, "Tell me then, I beg you, dear friend!

Tell me, as it cannot be otherwise, that you too, my learned friend, are going to make your appeal to the sublime Buddha!"

Siddhartha lay his hand on Govinda's shoulder: "You have not heard my wish for your success, o Govinda. I will repeat it: May you follow this path to its end. May you find deliverance!"

At this moment Govinda understood that his friend was leaving him, and he began to weep.

"Siddhartha!" he called out in a lamenting tone.

Siddhartha spoke to him amiably: "Do not forget, Govinda, that now you belong to the shramanas of the Buddha! You have renounced your home and your parents, you have renounced your origin and your property, renounced your own will, renounced friendship. This is the will of the teachings. This is the will of the Exalted One. This is your own will. Tomorrow, o Govinda, I shall leave you."

For a long time still the friends wandered in the grove, for a long time they lay and found no sleep. And over and over Govinda pressed his friend, he wanted Siddhartha to tell him why he would not take refuge in Gautama's teachings, what error he found in the teachings. But each time Siddhartha declined to answer and said: "Rest content, Govinda! The teachings of the Exalted One are most excellent, how shall I find a single error in them?"[29]

At the very break of day a follower of the Buddha, one of his oldest monks, walked through the garden and called to him every neophyte who had taken refuge in the teachings, giving each one the yellow robe to don and instruction in the first precepts and duties of his station. Then Govinda tore himself away, embraced the friend of his youth once more and joined the train of novices.

Siddhartha, however, wandered in his thoughts through the grove.

Then Gautama came upon him, the Exalted One, and when he greeted him with reverence and the gaze of the Buddha was so full of quiet goodness, the youth summoned the courage to ask the Venerable One for permission to address him. Silently the Sublime One nodded to grant his request.[30]

Siddhartha spoke: "Yesterday, o Exalted One, I was permitted to hear your marvelous teachings. Together with my friend I came from afar to listen to your teachings. And now my friend will remain with your people, he has taken refuge with you. I, however, will set out on my pilgrimage anew."

"As you please," replied the Venerable One politely.

"My words are far too bold," Siddhartha continued, "but I would not like to leave the Exalted One without having conveyed to him my thoughts in all sincerity. Does the Venerable One wish to grant me another moment's audience?"

Silently the Buddha nodded his assent.

Siddhartha spoke: "There is one thing, o most Venerable One, that I admire above all else in your teachings. Everything in your teachings is completely clear, is demonstrated; you show the world as a single eternal chain, joined by cause and effect, as one perfect chain that is never and nowhere broken.[31] Never has this been seen so clearly, never so irrefutably described; the heart of each Brahmin must truly beat higher in his breast when he, through your teachings, perceives the world as perfectly coherent, unbroken, clear as crystal, not dependent on chance, not dependent on the gods. Whether good or evil, whether worldly life may be suffering or joy, let that remain undecided, perhaps this does not matter—but the unity of the world, the coherence of occurrence, the enclosure of everything great and small by the same stream, by the same law of causes, of genesis and of death, this shines brightly from your sublime teachings, o Perfect One. But now, according to your same teachings, this unity and logical consistency of all things nonetheless is interrupted at one place, and through one small breach in this world of unity something strange, something new, something that did not previously exist and that can neither be shown nor proven streams in: this is your teaching of the overcoming of the world, of deliverance. With this small gap, with this small breach the entire eternal and universal law is again broken and annulled. Please forgive me for uttering this objection."[32]

Quietly Gautama had listened to him, unmoved. With his kindly, his polite and clear voice now the Perfect One spoke: "You have heard the teachings, o Brahmin's son, and good for you that you have reflected so deeply. You have found a gap, an error. You are welcome to contemplate further. But be warned, hungry as you are for knowledge, beware of the thicket of opinion and the battle over words. This has nothing to do with opinions, they may be lovely or hateful, clever or idiotic, each of us can hang on to them or dispense with them. But the teachings that you have heard from me are not opinion, and their goal is not to explain the world to those who hunger for knowledge. They have another goal: their goal is deliverance from suffering. This is what Gautama teaches, nothing else."[33]

"I do not wish for you, o Exalted One, to be angry with me," said the youth. "It was not because I sought to fight with you, to quarrel over words, that I spoke to you like that. Indeed, you are right, little is a matter of opinion. But allow me to say one thing more: Not for one moment have I doubted you. I have not doubted for a moment that you are Buddha, that you have attained the goal, the highest goal toward which so many thousands of Brahmins and sons of Brahmins are on the path. You have found deliverance from death. It has come to you out of your own seeking, on your own path, through thinking, through meditation, through knowledge, through enlightenment. It has not come to you through teaching! And—such is my thinking, o Exalted One—no one attains deliverance through teaching![34] To no one, o most Venerable One, will you be able to speak and convey in words what happened in the hour of your enlightenment! The teachings of the enlightened Buddha encompass a great deal, they teach much, how to live life righteously, how to avoid evil. But one thing the teachings, so clear and so venerable, do not contain: they do not contain the secret of what the Exalted One himself experienced, he alone among the hundreds of thousands. This is what I was thinking and recognized when I listened to the teachings. This is the reason on account of which I intend to continue my journey—not to seek out some other, better instruction, for I know there is none, rather to leave all teachings and all teachers and alone attain my goal or else die. Oftentimes, however, I shall think of this day, o Exalted One, and of this hour, when my eyes beheld a holy man."

The eyes of the Buddha gazed tranquilly at the ground, his inscrutable countenance radiated stillness and complete equanimity.

"May your thoughts," the Venerable One spoke slowly, "not be missteps! May you reach your goal! But tell me: Have you seen my troop of shramanas, my many brothers who have taken refuge in the teachings? And do you think, alien shramana, do you believe that it would be better for all of them to abandon the teachings and to return to the life of the world and of the passions?"[35]

"Far is such a thought from me," Siddhartha cried. "My wish is that they all remain with the teachings, may they all reach their goal! It is not my place to judge the life of another! Only for myself, for myself alone must I judge, must I choose, must I decline. Deliverance from the I is what we shramanas seek, o Exalted One. Were I one of your disciples, o Venerable One, I fear it might happen that only through semblance and deception would my I find rest and be released, but that in truth it would live on and grow large, for then I would have absorbed the teachings, my emulation of you, my love for you, for the entire community of monks into my I!"

With half a smile, with an unwavering brightness and amiability Gautama looked the stranger in the eye and bade him farewell with a scarcely visible gesture.

"Clever you are, o Shramana," said the Venerable One. "You know how to speak cleverly, my friend. Be on guard against too much cleverness!"

Away walked the Buddha, and his gaze and his half smile were forever engraved on Siddhartha's memory.

I have still not seen a human being look or smile, sit or walk that way, he thought; I, too, wish to be capable of gazing and smiling so truly, of sitting and walking so freely, so venerably, so cryptically, so openly, so like a child and full of secrets. Only a human being who has penetrated his innermost self gazes and walks so truly. Well, I too shall seek to penetrate the innermost part of my self.

There is one human being I have seen, Siddhartha thought, one single man before whom I had to cast down my eyes. Before no one else do I want to look down anymore, for no one else. No other teachings will ever entice me, since this man's teachings did not tempt me.

He has robbed me, the Buddha, Siddhartha thought, he has robbed me, and yet he has given me a greater gift. He has robbed me of my friend, who believed in me and who now believes in him, who was my shadow and now is Gautama's shadow. But he has given me the gift of Siddhartha, my self.

# AWAKENING

When Siddhartha left the grove, in which the Buddha, the Perfect One, remained, in which Govinda remained, then he felt that the life he had lived until that time also remained behind him in the grove, separate from him. He brooded on this perception, which filled him completely, as he slowly went along. Deeply he brooded, as if lowering himself through deep water even to the bottom of this perception, even to that place where the causes rest, for it seemed to him that this is precisely what thought is about—apprehension of causes, through this alone do perceptions become insights, they are not lost, rather they become real and start to glow with what is within them.

Walking along slowly Siddhartha turned and brooded. He recognized that he was no longer a youth but had become a man. He was aware that he had been deserted, as the snake is deserted by its shed skin, that something was no longer available to him, something that had been with him and belonged to him all through his youth: the wish to have a teacher and to be taught. He had relinquished the last teacher who had appeared to him on his path, even him, the highest and wisest teacher, the most Holy One, Buddha, he had to part from him, he had not been able to accept his teachings.

More slowly the thinker proceeded, asking himself: "But what *is* it you wanted to learn from the teachings and teachers, and those who taught you so much, what could they not teach you?" And he concluded: "It was the I, whose meaning and essence I wanted to learn. It was the I, from which I wanted release, which I wanted to conquer. But I could not conquer it, I could only deceive it, only flee from it, only hide myself from it. Truly, nothing in the world has taken up so much of my thinking as this I of mine, this conundrum, that I am alive, that I am one and separate and cut off from everyone else, that I am Siddhartha! And about nothing in the world do I know less than about me, about Siddhartha!"

Seized by this thought, the thinker who was slowly walking along stopped still, and from this thought another immediately sprang, a new notion, which ran as follows: "That I know nothing of myself, that Siddhartha has remained so alien and unknown to me, this comes from a cause, from one single cause: I was afraid of myself, I was fleeing myself! I was seeking Atman, I was seeking Brahman, I was determined to carve up my I and peel it apart, in order to find in its unknown interior what was at the core of all husks, to find Atman, life, the divine, the ultimate. I myself, however, got lost in the process."

Siddhartha opened his eyes and looked around him, a smile filled his face, and a deep sensation of awakening from long dreams streamed through him even into his toes. And instantly his pace quickened, he walked briskly, like a man who knows what he has to do.

"Oh," he thought breathing freely, taking a deep breath, "I will not let Siddhartha slip away from me now! No longer do I want my thinking and my life to begin with Atman and the suffering of the world. No longer do I want to slay and dismember myself, to find a secret behind the remains. Neither Yoga Veda nor Atharva Veda shall instruct me, neither the ascetics nor any other teachers. In the school of myself I want to learn, that is where I want to be a pupil, I want to get to know myself, the secret that is Siddhartha."

He looked around, as if he were seeing the world for the first time. The world was beautiful, the world was particolored, strange and quizzical. Here was blue, here was yellow, here green, the sky flowed and the river, the forest froze with the mountains, everything beautiful, everything full of mystery and magic, and in its midst he, Siddhartha, the awakening one, on the way to himself. All this, all this yellow and blue, river and forest for the first time entered through his eyes, no longer Mara's magic, no longer the veil of Maya, no longer the pointless and random multiplicity of the world of appearance, contemptible to the deep-thinking Brahmin, who scorns multiplicity, who seeks unity.[36] Blue was blue, river was river, and if the one and the divine also lay concealed in the blue and in the river and in Siddhartha, it was just the nature and meaning of the divine to be yellow here, blue here, there sky, there forest and here Siddhartha.[37] Meaning and essence were not somewhere behind things, they were inside things, in everything.

"How deaf I have been, how stupid!" he thought as he walked quickly. "When someone reads a text whose meaning he wants to comprehend, he does not despise the signs and letters, calling them deceptive, contingent, and worthless husks, but rather he reads them, he studies and loves them, letter by letter. But I, the I who wished to read the book of the world and the book of my own essential being, I have, for the sake of a previously imagined meaning, held these signs and letters in contempt, calling the world of appearances deception, calling my eye and my tongue themselves contingent and worthless appearances. No, this is over, I have awakened, I have indeed awakened and today is the first day of my new life."

While Siddhartha was thinking these thoughts, again he suddenly halted, stopped still, as if a snake lay on the path ahead of him.

Because suddenly this too was clear to him: He, who indeed was like one who had been awakened or newborn, he had utterly to begin his life over from the very beginning. That same morning when he had left the Jetavana, the grove of the Exalted One, already awakening, already on the path to himself, it was his intention and it seemed natural and self-evident that he, after the years of his asceticism, would return to his birthplace and to his father. But now, in the very moment that he stood there, as if a snake lay in his path, he also awakened to this insight: "I am no longer who I was, I am no longer an ascetic, I am no longer a priest, I am no longer a Brahmin. What then should I do back home in my father's house? Study? Perform sacrifices? Practice meditation? All this is past, none of this is on my path any longer."

Siddhartha stood motionless; for a moment, for the length of one breath his heart froze, he felt it freeze inside his chest like a small animal, a bird or a hare, as he saw how alone he was. For years he had been without a home and had not felt it. Now he felt it. Up until now, even in the depths of meditative absorption, he had been his father's son, a Brahmin, of high caste, a spiritual man. Now he was only Siddhartha, the one who had awakened, nothing more. Deeply he drew in his breath and for a moment he froze and stood shuddering. No one was as alone as he. No one of noble birth who did not belong among the other nobles, no artisan who did not feel fellowship with other artisans and find refuge with them, share their life, speak their language. No Brahmin who did not count himself a Brahmin and live with them, no ascetic who did not find himself and take refuge in the shramanas' caste; even the most forlorn hermit in the forest was not one and alone, community surrounded him, he too belonged to a caste, which was home to him. Govinda had become a monk, and thousands of monks were his brothers, wore his garment, believed his beliefs, spoke his language. But he, Siddhartha, where did he fit in? Whose life would he share? Whose language would he speak?

Out of this moment, where the world melted away all around him, where he appeared as the sole star in the sky, out of this moment of chill and dejection, Siddhartha emerged, more I than before, more tightly gathered in. He felt: This had been the last shudder of awakening, the final convulsion of birth. And instantly he set out again, starting to walk quickly and impatiently, no longer toward home, no longer to his father, no longer back.

*Part Two*

# KAMALA

Siddhartha learned something new on every step of his path, for the world was transformed, and his heart was spellbound. He saw the sun rise over wooded highlands and set over distant shores that were lined with palms. At night he saw stars arranged in the heavens, and the crescent moon floating like a boat in the blue. He saw trees, stars, beasts, clouds, rainbows, rocks, plants, flowers, stream and river, morning dew flashing in the underbrush, high distant mountains blue and pale, birds singing and bees, wind blowing silver-toned in the rice paddy. This all, all this, thousandfold and particolored, had always been there, the sun and moon had always shone, always the rivers had rushed and the bees buzzed, but that was in former times when, for Siddhartha, all this had been nothing but a transient and illusory veil before his eyes, to be regarded with distrust, destined to be pierced by thought and utterly destroyed, for it was not essence—essence lay beyond the visible. Now, however, his vision had cleared and lingered here, on this side, it saw and acknowledged the visible; it sought home in this world, not seeking essence, not setting its sights on the beyond. The world was beautiful when regarded like this, without searching, so simply, in such a childlike way. Moon and stars were beautiful, beautiful were bank and stream, forest and rocks, goat and gold-bug, flower and butterfly. So lovely, so delightful to go through the world this way, so like a child, awake, open to what is near, without distrust. The sun's heat on one's head felt different, the cool shade of the woods felt different, water from the brook and cistern tasted different, as did the pumpkin and banana. Short were the days, short the nights, each hour fled swiftly as a sail on the sea, under that sail a ship full of treasures, full of joys. Siddhartha saw a tribe of monkeys wandering in the high forest canopy, high in the branches, heard their wild, avid singing. Siddhartha saw a ram trail a ewe and mate with her. In a reedy lake at evening time he saw a hungry pike hunt its prey; anxiously hurrying ahead of it multitudes of small fry sparkled and flip-flopped out of the water, the scent of power and passion rushed urgently out of whirlpools stirred up by the pike in tumultuous chase.

All this had always been there, and he had not seen it; he had not been present. Now he was present, he belonged there. Through his eyes coursed light and shadow, through his heart stars and moon.

Along the way Siddhartha also remembered everything he had experienced in the Jetavana garden, the teachings he had heard there, the divine Buddha, taking leave of Govinda, his own conversation with the Exalted One. Again he recalled the words he had spoken to the Exalted One, every single one of them, and inside he was astonished that back then he had said things he really had no idea he knew. What he had said to Gautama: That the Buddha's secret treasure was not his teachings, but rather the inexpressible, what could not be taught, what he had once learned in the hour of his enlightenment—this is what it was, what he was now distilling from experience, what he was now beginning to experience. He had to experience himself now. Of course he had long known that his self was Atman, of the same eternal essence as Brahman. But never had he truly found this self, for he had wanted to catch it with the net of thought. Surely neither was the body the self, nor the play of the mind, neither was it the imagination, nor reason, nor received wisdom, nor the learned art of drawing inferences and of thus spinning new thoughts from old. No, even this world of thought was still here on this side, and slaying the contingent I of the senses only to fatten the contingent I of thought and erudition led nowhere. Thought and the senses both were delightful things, the ultimate meaning lay hidden behind both, it was essential to heed both, to play with both, neither to scorn nor overestimate either one, to listen closely to both for their secret innermost voices. He would strive for nothing, except for that which the voice commanded him to strive; nowhere would he linger, except where the voice advised. Why was Gautama sitting under the bodhi tree just then, at the hour of hours, when enlightenment came to him? He had heard a voice, a voice in his own heart, which commanded him to seek rest under that tree, and he preferred neither mortification, nor sacrifice, neither bathing nor prayer, food nor drink, neither sleep nor dreams, he obeyed the voice. So to obey, not an external command, only the voice, to be ready in that way, this was good, this was necessary, nothing else was necessary.[1]

In the night, as he slept in the straw hut of a ferryman beside the river, Siddhartha had a dream: Govinda stood before him, wearing the yellow robe of the ascetic. Govinda looked sad, sadly he asked: Why have you left me? Then he embraced Govinda, wrapped his arms around him, and while he drew him to his breast and kissed him, it ceased to be Govinda, rather it was a woman, and from the woman's gown emerged a full breast streaming with milk, at which Siddhartha lay and drank; sweet and strong tasted the milk of this breast. It had the taste of woman and man, sun and forest, beast and blossom, of every fruit, of every desire. Intoxicating, leaving him senseless.—When Siddhartha awakened, the pale river shimmered through the hut's doorway, and deep in the woods the euphonious dark call of an owl sounded.

As the day began, Siddhartha asked his host the ferryman to take him across the river.[2] The ferryman took him across the river on his bamboo raft; the broad water had a reddish sheen in the morning light.

"What a beautiful river this is," he said to his escort.

"Yes," said the ferryman, "a very beautiful river, I love it above all else. Often I have listened to it, often I have looked into its eyes, and I have always learned from it. One can learn a great deal from a river."

"Let me offer thanks, dear patron," Siddhartha declared, when he set foot on the opposite bank. "I have no token of gratitude for you,

my host, and nothing with which to pay you. I am homeless, the son
of a Brahmin, and a shramana."

"I could see that myself," said the ferryman, "I did not expect
payment or any token from you. You will give me a gift some other
time."

"Do you think so?" Siddhartha said with amusement.

"Certainly. This too I have learned from the river: Everything
returns! You, too, Shramana, will come back. Now, farewell! May
your friendship be my reward. Think of me when you sacrifice to
the gods!"

Smiling, they took their leave. Smiling, Siddhartha was pleased
with their friendship and the ferryman's congeniality. "How like
Govinda he is," he thought with a smile, "all the people I meet along
the way are like Govinda. All of them are thankful, though they
themselves deserve thanks. All are obsequious, all would like to be
friends, to obey, to think as little as possible. People are children."

Around midday he passed through a village. Children ran
around in the alleys in front of some mud huts, playing with
pumpkin seeds and seashells, screaming and scuffling, but they
all ran away, shy of the strange shramana. Where the village
ended the path crossed a brook, and at the edge of the brook a
young woman kneeled, washing clothing. When Siddhartha
greeted her, she raised her head and looked up at him with a
smile; he could see the dazzling whites of her eyes. He called out
a blessing, as is the custom among travelers, and asked how far it
was to the next city. Then she stood up and walked over to him;
her mouth was moist and beautiful, glistening in her young face.
She bantered with him, asked whether he had eaten yet, whether
it was true that shramanas slept alone in the woods at night and
were not permitted to have women with them. While doing this
she set her left foot against his right, making the move a woman
makes when inviting a man to engage in that manner of lovers'
delight the treatises call "climbing the tree." Siddhartha felt his
blood heat up, and since at this moment his dream came back to

him, he stooped over a little to the woman and with his lips kissed the brown tip of her breast. Looking up, he saw her smiling face full of desire and her eyes, made small, entreating him with longing.

Siddhartha, too, felt longing, felt the root of his sex moving; but since he had never yet touched a woman, he hesitated a moment, just as his hands were on the verge of grasping her. And in this moment, trembling, he heard his innermost voice, and the voice said No. Then all the magic drained from the young woman's smiling face, and he saw nothing more than the moist gaze of an animal in heat. Amiably he stroked her cheek, turned on light feet and vanished from the sight of the disillusioned woman into the bamboo wood.

This same day, before evening he reached a city, and he was glad because he desired human company. He had lived in the forests for a long time, and the straw hut of the ferryman, in which he had spent the previous night, was the first roof he had had over his head in quite some time.

Outside the city, near a lovely grove enclosed by a fence, a small band of servants and serving maids, laden with baskets, met the wanderer. In their midst, carried by four of them, beneath the multicolored sun-roof of an ornate palanquin, a woman sat upon red cushions, their mistress. Siddhartha paused outside the entrance to the pleasure grove and watched the procession, beheld the servants, the maids, the baskets, the palanquin and, inside it, beheld the lady. Under her towering mass of black hair, he saw a very clear, very sweet, very clever face, a mouth bright red, like a fig freshly split open; her eyebrows groomed and painted as high arches, her dark eyes clever and watchful, her long delicate neck rose from a cloak of green and gold; her long, slender hands luminous, at rest, with broad gold bands circling their wrists.

Siddhartha saw how beautiful she was, and his heart laughed. He bowed low when the litter approached and straightening again, he gazed into the sweet, shining face, read for a moment her intelligent eyes with their high arched brows, breathed in a scent with which he was not familiar. Smiling, the lovely woman nodded, for just one moment, then she disappeared into the grove, and behind her the servants.

So I am entering this city, Siddhartha thought, under good auspices. The grove attracted him, pulling him in at once, but he thought better of it, and now he first grew conscious of how the servants and maids at the entrance had regarded him, with what contempt and suspicion, how dismissive they were.

I am still a shramana, he thought, still an ascetic and a beggar. I will not be permitted to remain so, not if I want to enter the grove. And he laughed.

He asked the next person who came along about the grove and the name of this woman, and he learned this was the grove of Kamala, the famous courtesan, and that beyond the grove she had a house in the city.[3]

Then he entered the city. Now he had a destination.

In pursuit of his goal, he allowed the city to drink him in, drifting in the stream of the alleys, stopping in the squares, resting on the stone stairs by the river. Toward evening he made friends with a barber's assistant, whom he had seen working in the shade of an archway, whom he found again praying in a temple to Vishnu, and to whom he told stories of Vishnu and Lakshmi. By the boats on the river he spent the night and early in the morning, before the first customers came to the shop, he had the barber's helper shave his beard and cut his hair, comb his hair and rub it with fine scented oil. Then he went to bathe in the river.

When late in the afternoon the beautiful Kamala seated in her palanquin drew near her grove, Siddhartha stood at the entrance, bowed to her and received the courtesan's greeting. But he waved to the young servant who was last in the train and bade him report to his mistress that a young Brahmin wished to speak with her. After a time, the servant returned, inviting the one who was waiting to follow him, conducting his follower silently into a pavilion where Kamala lay on a sofa, and left him alone with her.

"Was it not you outside there yesterday, standing there, greeting me?" Kamala asked.

"Indeed I did see you yesterday and I offered you my greeting."

"But did you not have a beard yesterday, and long hair, and dust in your hair?"

"Yes indeed that is what you observed, you saw everything. You saw Siddhartha, the son of a Brahmin, who had left his home in order to become a shramana and was a shramana for three years. But now I have left that track, and I came to the city, and the first thing I encountered, even before setting foot in the city, was you. I have come here to tell you this, o Kamala! You are the first woman to whom Siddhartha has spoken other than with downcast eyes. Never more do I want to cast down my eyes when I encounter a beautiful woman."

Kamala smiled and played with her peacock-feather fan. And she asked: "Siddhartha has come to me only to tell me this?"

"To tell you this, and to thank you for being so beautiful. And if it does not offend you, Kamala, I would like to ask you to be my friend and teacher, for as yet I know nothing of the art of which you are the mistress."

Then Kamala laughed out loud.

"Never before has this happened to me, Friend, that a shramana from the forest has come to me desiring instruction! Never has it happened to me, that a shramana with long hair and in an old torn loincloth has come to me! Many young men come to me, and even the sons of Brahmins are among them, but they come in fine clothing, they come in fine shoes, they have perfume in their hair and money in their purses. That is the condition in which they come, Shramana, the youths who come to me."

Siddhartha spoke: "I have already begun to learn from you. Even yesterday I already learned something. I got rid of my beard, had my hair combed and rubbed with oil. There is little that I still lack, most Splendid One: fine clothing, fine shoes, money in my purse. Know that Siddhartha has taken on things more difficult than such trivialities and has accomplished them. How should I not achieve what I made up my mind to do yesterday: to be your friend and to learn the joys of love from you! You will find me tractable, Kamala, far more difficult things have I learned than what you shall teach me. But tell me now: Siddhartha does not suffice you, as he is, with oil in his hair, but without clothing, without shoes, without money?"

Laughing, Kamala exclaimed, "No, my dear, he does not yet suffice. He must have clothing, lovely clothing, and shoes, lovely shoes, and lots of money in his purse, and gifts for Kamala. Do you understand now, Shramana from the forest? Can you bear all that in mind?"

"Indeed I can," exclaimed Siddhartha. "How could I not bear in mind what comes out of such a mouth! Your mouth is like a fig that has just split open, Kamala. My mouth is also red and fresh, it will suit yours, you will see.—But tell me, beautiful Kamala, have you no fear whatsoever of the shramana who has come out of the forest, who has come to learn the ways of love?"

"Why should I fear a shramana, a silly shramana from the forest, one who comes from the jackals and knows nothing of women?"

"O, the shramana is strong, and he fears nothing. He could take you by force, pretty girl. He could rob you. He could do you harm."

"No, Shramana, this I do not fear. Does a shramana or a Brahmin ever fear that someone will come and pounce on him and steal his erudition and his piety and his pensiveness? No, for these properly belong to him and he gives of them only as he likes and to whom he likes. That is how things stand with him; it is precisely the same for Kamala with the joys of love. Lovely and red is Kamala's mouth, but try to kiss it against Kamala's will and not a drop of sweetness will you have from it, which is so capable of dispensing great sweetness! You are intelligent, Siddhartha, so learn this too: Love can be begged, bought, received as a gift, found on the street, but it cannot be stolen. You have invented a way that is incorrect. No, it would be a pity if an attractive young man like yourself wanted to go about it the wrong way."

Siddhartha bowed and smiled. "It would be a shame, Kamala, how right you are! It would be a terrible shame. No, from your mouth to mine not a drop of sweetness will go astray, nor from mine to yours! But it remains for Siddhartha to return when he has what he still lacks: clothing, shoes, money. But tell me, lovely Kamala, could you give me one more piece of advice?"

"Advice? Why not? Who would not gladly give a piece of advice to a poor, ignorant shramana, who comes from the jackals in the forest?"

"Dear Kamala, advise me: where shall I go to most quickly find those three things?"

"Friend, many would like to know that. You must do what you have learned and allow people to give you money for it, and clothing, and shoes. Otherwise a poor person does not come into money. What can you do?"

"I can think. I can wait. I can fast."

"Nothing else?"

"Nothing. Oh yes, I can also compose poetry. Will you give me a kiss for a poem?"

"Yes, I will, if the poem pleases me. What is it called then?"

After a moment's deliberation, Siddhartha recited these lines:

Into her shadowy grove entered the lovely Kamala
At the grove's gateway stood the sun-brown shramana.
Deeply, beholding the lotus blossom,
Bowed the ascetic. With a smile she thanked him, Kamala.
Far more delightful, the youth thought, than offering to the gods,
Far more delightful to offer oneself to the lovely Kamala.

Kamala clapped her hands so loudly that her golden bracelets rang.

"Beautiful are your verses, sun-brown shramana, and truly, I will lose nothing if I give you a kiss in exchange."

She drew him toward her with her eyes, he inclined his face toward hers and lay his mouth on her mouth, which was like a freshly split-open fig. For a long time he kissed Kamala, and Siddhartha was filled with deep astonishment as she taught him how wise she was, how she ruled him, put him off, lured him back, and how behind this first row of kisses came another long, well-ordered, well-tested series, each one different from the other, still awaiting him. Breathing deeply, he remained standing and at this moment he was like a child astonished by the abundance of knowledge and things worth learning opening up before his eyes.

"Your verses are very beautiful," Kamala declared, "if I were rich, I would give you gold pieces for them. But it will be difficult for you to earn as much money as you need with verses. For you will need a lot of money if you want to be Kamala's friend."

"How you can kiss, Kamala!" Siddhartha stammered.

"Yes, I certainly can, that is why I do not lack clothing, shoes, bracelets and all sorts of lovely things. But what will become of you? Can you do nothing but think, fast, and make poems?"

"I also know the sacrificial songs," said Siddhartha, "but I no longer want to sing them. I also know magic formulae, but I no longer want to recite them. I have read the scriptures—"

"Stop," Kamala interrupted him. "You can read? And write?"[4]

"Certainly I can. Many people can."

"Most people cannot. Even I cannot. It is very good that you can read and write, very good. You will also be able to use the magic spells."

At this moment a serving maid came running and whispered some news into her mistress's ear.

"I have a visitor," Kamala cried. "You must leave here quickly, Siddhartha, bear in mind that no one may see you here! Tomorrow I will see you again."

But she ordered the maid to give the pious Brahmin a white over-garment. Without knowing how it happened, Siddhartha saw himself snatched away by the maid, taken on a roundabout path into a garden house, given a caftan, conducted into the bushes and urgently admonished immediately to vanish from the grove unseen.

Contented, he did as he was told. Accustomed to the forest, he got himself out of the grove and over the hedge without a sound. Contented he returned to the city, carrying the rolled-up garment under his arm. He set himself outside the door of a hostel where travelers stopped to eat, asking silently for food, silently he accepted a piece of rice cake. Perhaps by tomorrow, he thought, I will no longer have to ask anyone for food.

Pride suddenly blazed up inside him. He was no longer a shramana, it was no longer appropriate for him to beg. He gave the rice cake to a dog and remained without food.

"Simple is the life that one leads here in the world," thought Siddhartha. "There are no obstacles. Everything was difficult, tiresome, and in the end hopeless while I was still a shramana. Now everything is easy, easy as the instruction in kissing Kamala gives me. I need clothing and money, nothing else, these are small goals and near; I won't lose any sleep over them."

Some time had passed since he had learned the location of Kamala's house in the city; the next day he went there and presented himself.

"It's all set," she called out to him. "You are expected at Kamaswami's, he is the wealthiest merchant in this city.[5] If he likes you, he will take you into his service. Be clever, sun-brown shramana. I have let him hear about you through others. Be friendly toward him, he is very powerful. But do not be too modest! I do not want you to become his servant, you should become his equal, otherwise I will not be happy with you. Kamaswami is beginning to grow old and comfortable. If he likes you, he will entrust a great deal to you."

Siddhartha thanked her and laughed, and when she learned that he had not eaten that day or the day before, she had bread and fruits brought to him, providing him with a feast.

"You have had luck," she said in parting, "one door after another has opened for you. How does this happen? Do you have a magic charm?"

Siddhartha replied: "Yesterday I told you the story of my understanding how to think, wait, and fast, but you found this all of no use. But these things are of great use, Kamala, as you will see. You will see that the silly shramanas in the forest teach and know many fine things that you do not. The day before yesterday I was a scraggly beggar, yesterday I already kissed Kamala, and soon I will be a merchant and have money for all the things you hold in esteem."

"Yes, now that is true," she admitted. "But how would things be for you without me? Where would you be if Kamala had not helped you?"

"Dear Kamala," Siddhartha said, straightening himself to his full height, "when I came to you in your grove, I took the first step. It was my purpose to learn love from the loveliest of women. From the very moment that I grasped my purpose, I also knew I would carry it out. I knew you would help me, from your first gaze at the entrance of the grove I already knew it."

"But if I had not wanted to?"

"You *did* want to. Look, Kamala: When you throw a stone into water, it hurries the quickest way down to the bottom of the water. So it is when Siddhartha has a goal, a purpose. Siddhartha does nothing, he waits, he thinks, he fasts, but he passes through the things of the world as the stone passes through the water, without doing anything, without touching anything; he is pulled, he lets himself fall. His goal pulls him toward it, for he admits nothing into his soul that would resist the goal. This is what Siddhartha learned among the shramanas. This is what fools call magic and what they think of as the work of demons. Nothing is done by demons, there are no demons. Anyone can work magic, anyone can reach his goals, if he can think, if he can wait, if he can fast."

Kamala listened to him. She loved his voice, she loved the gaze of his eyes.

"Maybe, Friend," she said gently, "what you say is so. Maybe it is also the case that Siddhartha is a handsome man, that his gaze pleases women, and that is why good fortune comes to him."

With a kiss Siddhartha parted from her. "May it be so, my teacher. May my gaze always please you, may good fortune always come to me from you!"

# AMONG THE CHILD PEOPLE

Siddhartha went to see the merchant Kamaswami, he was shown into a prosperous residence; servants conducted him between valuable tapestries into a chamber, where he awaited the master of the house.

Kamaswami entered, a quick, lithe man with thick graying hair, with very clever, wary eyes, with a covetous mouth. Master and guest greeted each other amicably.

"I have been told," the merchant began, "that you are a Brahmin, a learned man, but that you are offering your services to a merchant. Have you fallen upon hard times, Brahmin, that you seek employment?"

"No," Siddhartha answered, "I have not fallen upon hard times, not now, not ever. Know then, that I come to you from the shramanas, among whom I have lived for a long time."

"If you come from among the shramanas, how can you be other than in need? Are not the shramanas entirely without possessions?"

"I have no possessions," said Siddhartha, "if that is what you mean. Certainly I have none. But I gave them up of my own free will, and thus I am in no distress."

"Then what will you live on, if you have no possessions?"

"I have never thought about it, Sir. I have been without possessions for more than three years, and I have never thought about what I should live on."

"So you have lived off the property of others."

"Presumably that is the case. The merchant too lives off the belongings of others."

"Well stated. But he does not take from those others what is theirs and give them nothing in return: he gives them his wares."

"That is indeed how it appears. Everyone takes, everyone gives, this is how life is."

"But permit me to ask: if you have no possessions, what then can you give?"

"Everyone gives what he has. The warrior gives strength, the merchant wares, the teacher instruction, the farmer rice, the fisherman fish."

"Very good. And now what is it that you have to give? What is it that you have learned, what knowledge do you possess?"

"I can think. I can wait. I can fast."

"Is that all?"

"Yes, I believe that is all!"

"And what use is it? For example fasting—what is it good for?"

"It is very good, Sir. If a person has nothing to eat, fasting is the most prudent course. If, for example, Siddhartha had not learned how to fast, today he would have had to accept some kind of—any kind of—employment, whether with you or somewhere else, because hunger would have driven him to it. But as it is Siddhartha can wait calmly, he knows no impatience, he knows no distress, he can let hunger besiege him for a long time and laugh as well. For that reason, Sir, fasting is good."

"You are right, Shramana. Wait a moment."

Kamaswami went out and returned with a scroll, which he handed over to his guest, while asking, "Can you read this?"

Siddhartha examined the scroll, on which a deed of sale was recorded, and he began to read it aloud.

"Excellent," said Kamaswami. "And will you write something on this sheet for me?"

He gave him paper and a stylus, and Siddhartha wrote and gave the page back to him.

Kamaswami read: "Writing is good, thinking is better. Cleverness is good, patience is better."

"Your comprehension of writing is superior," the merchant praised him. "We still have many things to discuss together. For today, I invite you to be my guest and take up residence in this house."

Siddhartha thanked him and accepted, and now lived in the house of the businessman. Clothes were brought to him, and shoes, and a servant prepared a bath for him daily. Twice a day a sumptuous meal was served, but Siddhartha ate only once a day, and neither did he eat flesh nor did he drink wine. Kamaswami told him about his business, showed him merchandise and warehouses, showed him accounting. Siddhartha learned a great deal that was new, he listened a lot and spoke little. Mindful of Kamala's words, he never subordinated himself to the merchant, they compelled him to deal with him as his equal, as more than his equal. Kamaswami pursued his business interests with great solicitude and often with passion, but Siddhartha regarded it all as a game whose rules he took pains to learn precisely, but whose substance did not touch his heart.

He was not long in Kamaswami's house when he began to participate in his master's trade. But daily at the hour when she called him, he visited the lovely Kamala, in handsome clothing, in fine shoes, and soon he also brought presents along with him. Her clever red mouth taught him a lot. Her tender, supple hand taught him a lot. He was still a boy when it came to love, one who besides tended blindly and rapaciously to plunge into pleasure as into a bottomless abyss, and she taught him from the ground up: that one cannot take pleasure without giving pleasure, and that every gesture, every stroke, every touch, every look, each minute point of the body has its mystery, the awakening of which gives joy to the initiated. She taught him that after a celebration of love, lovers dare not part without first admiring each other, without being conquered precisely as they themselves have conquered, so that in neither of the two may satiation or barrenness arise or the bad feeling of having abused or having been abused. Delightful were the hours he spent with the lovely and clever artist, becoming her student, her paramour, her friend. The value and meaning of his present life lay here with Kamala, not in Kamaswami's trade.

The merchant assigned the writing of important letters and contracts to him, and became accustomed to discussing all matters of importance with him. He soon saw that Siddhartha understood little about rice and wool, about shipping and trade, but that he had a lucky hand, and that Siddhartha surpassed him, the merchant, in calm and equanimity and in the art of listening to strangers and penetrating their mentality. "This Brahmin," he remarked to a friend, "is no real salesman and will never be one; his soul is never passionately involved in trade. But he has the secret of those to whom success comes of its own accord, whether he was born under a lucky star, whether it is magic, or something he learned among the shramanas. He always seems only to play at business, it never gets into his blood, it never rules him, he never fears failure, losses never bother him."

The merchant's friend advised him: "From the business he himself transacts, give him a third of the profits; when there are losses, however, let him take the same proportion of those losses. Then he will grow more keen."

Kamaswami followed the advice. Siddhartha, however, was little troubled by these matters. If he had profits, he pocketed them with equanimity; if he met with loss, he laughed and said: "Oh, my goodness, this has gone very badly!"

Actually he seemed indifferent to business affairs. Once he traveled to a village in order to buy up a large crop of rice. When he arrived, however, the rice had already been sold to another tradesman. Nonetheless Siddhartha stayed for some days in this village, regaled the farmers, gave their children copper coins, celebrated a wedding with them, and returned from the journey extremely content. Kamaswami reproached him for not having turned around immediately, saying he had wasted both time and money. Siddhartha answered: "Stop scolding, dear Friend! Scolding never accomplished anything. If you have lost money, allow me to absorb the loss. I am very satisfied with this journey. I have made many new acquaintances, a Brahmin has become my friend, children rode on my knee, farmers showed me their fields, nobody took me for a tradesman."

"How nice all this is," Kamaswami admitted reluctantly, "but I should like to say, the fact is you are nevertheless a tradesman! Or did you make the journey for your own pleasure alone?"

"Certainly," laughed Siddhartha, "certainly I traveled for my own pleasure. Why else do it? I got to know people and places, I enjoyed amiability and confidences, I made friends. You see, dear Kamaswami, if I were you, as soon as I would have seen my purchase thwarted, full of annoyance, I would have hurried back home, and then time and money would indeed have been lost. But instead I have had good days, I learned, I enjoyed myself, I harmed neither myself nor others through vexation or excessive haste. And if ever I go back that way again, perhaps to purchase a subsequent harvest, or for any purpose whatsoever, friendly people will receive me amiably and cheerfully, and I will have myself to commend for that, for not having shown haste and displeasure previously. So, Friend, leave well enough alone, it does you no good to scold! When the day comes on which you see: This Siddhartha does me no good, then say the word, and Siddhartha will go his way. But until then, let us be content with each other."

In vain, too, were the merchant's attempts to convince Siddhartha that he ate his, Kamaswami's, bread. Siddhartha ate his own bread, even more the two ate the bread of others, the bread of all. Never did Siddhartha lend an ear to Kamaswami's worries, and Kamaswami worried a lot. If some business affair threatened to fail, if a letter of transmission seemed to be lost, if a debtor seemed unable to pay, Kamaswami could never convince his colleague that it paid to waste words of distress or anger, to have a furrowed brow, to lose sleep. Once when Kamaswami was lecturing Siddhartha that he had learned everything he knew from him, he got in answer: "Would you please stop trying to make fun of me with such jokes! From you I have learned the price of a basket of fish and how much interest one can demand when one lends money. This is your science. From you, dear Kamaswami, I have not learned how to think; you should rather learn that from me."

His soul was indeed not in trade. Business was good—it brought in money for Kamala, and it brought in far more than he needed. For the rest, Siddhartha's interest and curiosity was only in people whose dealings, handiwork, troubles, delights and foolishness previously were as remote from and alien to him as the moon. As easily as he succeeded in speaking with everyone, in living with everyone, in learning from everyone, just as much was he nevertheless conscious that something separated him from them, and this separator was his shramanahood. He saw people living their lives in childlike or bestial ways, which he loved and scorned at one and the same time. He saw them take pains, saw them suffer and go gray over things that to him seemed unworthy of the price, over money, over small pleasures, trivial honors, he saw them chide and insult one another; he saw them lament over woes at which a shramana smiles, and suffer privations a shramana simply does not feel.

He was open to everything these people brought to him. Welcome to him was the dealer who offered to sell him linen, welcome was the debtor who came seeking a loan, welcome the beggar who for an hour wanted to tell him the story of his poverty, and who was not half so poor as any given shramana. He treated the rich foreign dealer no differently than the servant who shaved him, or the street vendor he allowed to swindle him out of small change when he bought bananas. If Kamaswami came to him to complain about his troubles or to reproach him concerning a business matter, he listened with eagerness and good cheer, was surprised at him, tried to understand him, let him have his way a little, just as much as seemed absolutely necessary, and turned away from him to the next person who demanded his attention. And many came to him, many to trade with him, many to cheat him, many to sound him out, many to call upon his compassion, many to seek his advice. He gave advice, he was compassionate, he gave gifts, he allowed himself to be cheated a little, and this entire game and the passion with which people played it occupied his thoughts just as much as the gods and Brahman had once occupied them.

At times, deep within his breast, he perceived a voice, dying, soft, a voice that gently admonished, gently lamented, scarcely so that he heard it. Then for an hour it came to his consciousness that he led a peculiar life, that he only did things that were nothing but a game, that although he felt cheerful and sometimes even felt joy, real life nonetheless flowed past him and did not touch him. Like a juggler juggling balls, so he played with matters of business, with the people around him, looked at them, found his amusement in them; with his heart, with the source of his essential being, he was not present. The source, the wellspring, ran somewhere or other, far from him, running and flowing invisibly, it had nothing more to do with his life. And several times he was terrified by such thoughts and wished it might also be vouchsafed him passionately and cordially to be involved in all the childish tasks of daily life, truly to live, truly to act, truly to enjoy life, instead of just standing by as an observer.

But still he returned to the lovely Kamala, learned the art of love, practiced the cult of pleasure, where more than anywhere else giving and taking became one, chatted with her, learned from her, gave her advice, took her advice. She understood him better, better than Govinda had once understood him, she was more like him.

Once he said to her: "You are like me, you are different from most people. You are Kamala, nothing else, and inside you is a stillness and a refuge, into which you can enter at any time and be at home, just as I can.[6] Few people have this, and yet everyone is capable of having this."

"Not all people are smart," Kamala replied.

"No," said Siddhartha, "that is not what this is about. Kamaswami is just as smart as I am, and yet has no refuge in himself. Others have it, who are small children when it comes to understanding. Most people, Kamala, are like falling leaves, which blow and turn in the air, and stagger and tumble to the ground. But others, fewer, are like stars, they travel in a fixed orbit, no wind reaches them, in themselves they have their law and their course. Among all the scholars and shramanas, of whom I knew many, was one of this type, a Perfect One, I can never forget him. That is the one called Gautama, the Exalted One, the prophet of the teachings. A thousand disciples hear his teaching every day, every hour they follow his precepts, but they are all falling leaves, in themselves they do not have the teachings and the law."

Kamala regarded him with a smile. "Again you are speaking of him," she said, "again you are having the thoughts of a shramana."

Siddhartha was silent, and they played the game of love, one of the thirty or forty different games Kamala knew. Her body was limber as that of a jaguar, and it bent like the huntsman's bow; whosoever learned love from her was versed in many pleasures, many secrets. She played with Siddhartha a long time, enticed him, rebuffed him, coerced him, embraced him, rejoiced in his masterliness, until he was vanquished and rested, exhausted, by her side.

The hetaera leaned over him, looked into his face for a long time, into his eyes which had grown tired.

"You are the best lover," she said pensively, "I have ever had. You are stronger than others, more flexible, more willing. You have learned my art well, Siddhartha. Someday, when I am older, I want to have your child. And nonetheless, my love, you have remained a shramana, nonetheless you do not love me, you love no human being. Is this not so?"

"It may well be so," Siddhartha said wearily. "I am like you. You do not love either—how could you practice love as an art otherwise? People of our kind may not be able to love. Child people can love; that is their secret."

# SAMSARA

For a long time Siddhartha had lived the life of the world and its pleasures, still without belonging to it. His senses, which he had mortified during his fervent shramana years, were awake again, he had tasted wealth, tasted lust, tasted power; nonetheless, for a long time in his heart he had remained a shramana, the wise Kamala correctly recognized this. His life still was guided by the art of thinking, of waiting, of fasting; still, people of the world, the child people, remained strange to him, just as he did to them.

Years went by; swathed in well-being, Siddhartha scarcely felt them fade. He had become rich, he long owned his own home with servants and a garden outside the city, by the river. People liked him, they came to him when they needed money or advice, but no one was close to him, no one but Kamala.

That high, bright alertness he had once experienced at the peak of his youth, in the days after hearing Gautama's sermon, after his separation from Govinda, that intent anticipation, that pride in standing alone with neither teachings nor a teacher, that pliant readiness to hear the divine voices in his own heart, had gradually become memory, had been transitory;[7] distant and soft rushed the holy wellspring, which once had been near, once rushing within his own self. Certainly a great deal that he had learned from the shramanas, that he had learned from Gautama, that he had learned from his father the Brahmin, remained in him a long time: modest living, joy in thinking, hours of meditation, secret knowledge of the self, of the eternal I, which is neither corpus nor consciousness. Some of this had remained in him, one thing after the other, however, had sunk down and been covered with dust. Like a potter's wheel, once set in motion, it turns a long time and only slowly wearies and slackens, so in Siddhartha's soul the wheel of asceticism, the wheel of thinking, the wheel of determination long continued to whirl, kept on spinning, but it spun slowly and hesitantly and nearly came to a standstill. Slowly, the way moisture penetrates a dying tree trunk, slowly filling it and making it rot, the material world and indolence had entered Siddhartha's soul, slowly filling it, weighing it down, making it weary, lulling it to sleep. In return his senses had come to life, much had they learned, much had they experienced.

Siddhartha had learned how to do business, how to wield power over people, how to amuse himself with women, he had learned to wear handsome clothing, to command servants, to bathe in fragrant waters. He had learned to eat carefully prepared delicacies, even fish and flesh and fowl, condiments and sweets, and to drink wine that makes one listless and forgetful. He had learned to play at dice and at the checkerboard, to look at dancing girls, to be carried in a palanquin, to sleep on a soft bed. But still he felt he was different from others and superior to them, he always looked down on them with some contempt, scornful contempt, the very contempt a shramana continually feels for men of the world. Whenever Kamaswami felt poorly, if he was irritable, if he felt offended, if he was tormented by the woes of commerce, Siddhartha had always regarded such displays with scorn. Only slowly and imperceptibly, with the passing harvest times and rainy seasons, his scorn had grown wearier, his superiority more quiescent. Only slowly, amidst his growing riches, Siddhartha himself had adopted something of the nature of the child people, something of their childishness and of their scruples. And yet he envied them, the more he resembled them, the more he envied them. He envied them the one thing he lacked and they had, the importance they were able to attribute to their lives, the passion of their joys and fears, the fearful but sweet bliss of their eternal amorousness. These people incessantly fell in love with themselves, their women, their children, with honor or money, plans or hopes. But he did not learn this from them, not even this, this childish joy and childish folly; what he learned directly from them was something unpleasant, something he himself felt contempt for. More and more often it happened that the morning after a sociable evening he lay about for quite some time feeling dull and tired. It happened that he became irritable and impatient when Kamaswami bored him with his troubles. It happened that he laughed all too loudly when he lost at dice. His face was still shrewder and more intelligent than other faces, but it seldom laughed, and one after another it took on those lineaments one so often finds in the faces of the rich, features of dissatisfaction, of infirmity, of discontent, of sluggishness, of uncharitableness. Slowly he was seized by the spiritual malaise of the rich.

Like a veil, like a thin mist, weariness settled upon Siddhartha, slowly, every day a bit thicker, every month a bit drearier, every year a bit heavier. As a new dress grows old with time, losing its lovely color, acquiring stains, acquiring folds, coming apart at the seams and starting to show awkward threadbare patches here and there, this is how Siddhartha's new life, which he had begun after separating from Govinda, had aged; this is how it lost its color and sheen with the years that were running out, this is how folds and stains gathered upon it, and basically hidden, here and there already hideously peering forth, disappointment and revulsion waited. Siddhartha did not notice this. He noticed only that his clear and certain innermost voice, which once had been awake inside him and always and ever guided him during his times of resplendence, that voice had gone silent.

The world held him captive, desire, covetousness, lassitude, and lastly even that vice he always considered the most foolish and which he had always held in the greatest contempt and scorned: avarice. Belongings, assets, and wealth in the end had captured him, this was no longer play, these were no longer frills, rather they had become a burden, he was chained to them. Siddhartha had gone astray on a strange path full of deceit owing to this last and most vile dependency, playing at dice. Since the time Siddhartha had ceased to be a shramana in his heart, he had begun to play the game for money and valuables—before then he had taken part casually and with a smile, as a custom of the child people—with increasing rage and passion. He was a formidable player, few wagered against him, so high and daring were his stakes. He played out of his heart's affliction, gambling away the wretched money and squandering it created a wrathful joy within him; in no other way could he show his contempt for wealth, for the idol of the merchants, more distinctly and with more disdain. So he rolled high and relentlessly, hating himself, taunting himself, he pocketed thousands, threw thousands away, gambled away money, jewels, a country house, then won again, lost again. That fear, that terrible and oppressive fear he felt while throwing the dice, while trembling over the high stakes, he loved that fear and always sought to refresh it, to increase it, to raise its level of titillation, for in this sensation alone did he still feel something like happiness, something like a rush of intoxication, something like heightened vigor in the midst of his satiated, tepid, insipid life. And after every great loss again he contemplated riches, returned more eagerly to business, pressed his debtors more harshly to pay, for he wanted to go on playing, he wanted to go on squandering, to go on showing his contempt for wealth. When he lost, Siddhartha lost his composure, he lost patience with those in default, lost his good will toward beggars, lost his desire to give and to lend money to those who came asking. He, who lost ten thousand on one roll of the dice and laughed, became more stringent and petty in his business dealings, and from time to time at night he dreamed of money! And as often as he awakened from this hideous enchantment, as often as he saw his face in the mirror on the bedroom wall grown older and more hideous, just as often shame and disgust assailed him, he fled further, fled into new games of chance, escaping into the anesthesia of lust, of wine, and from there back into the pursuit of accumulation and acquisition. In this senseless cycle he ran himself down, exhausting himself, growing old, growing sick.

Then one day a warning dream came to him. He had been with Kamala in the evening, in her beautiful pleasure garden. They were sitting under the trees, in conversation, and Kamala had spoken pensive words, words behind which mourning and weariness were concealed. She had asked him to tell her about Gautama and could not hear enough about him, how pure his eye, how still and lovely his mouth, how kind his smile, how peaceful his gait had been. He had to tell her tales about the exalted Buddha for a long time, and Kamala had sighed and had said, "Someday, perhaps soon, I too shall follow this Buddha. I shall give him my pleasure garden as a gift, and I will take my refuge in his teaching." After that though she had aroused him, and had shackled him to her in a game of love with such excruciating fervor, with biting and tears both, as if she wished once more to press the last sweet drops out of this vain, transitory lust. Never had it been so peculiarly clear to Siddhartha how closely lust is related to death. Then he had lain by her side, and Kamala's countenance had been close by, and beneath her eyes and near the corners of her mouth he had read, clearly as never before, an anxious script, a script of fine lines, of gentle furrows, a script that reminded him of autumn and old age, as then even Siddhartha himself, who was now some forty years old, had already noticed some graying hairs dispersed among his own black ones. Weariness was written upon Kamala's lovely face, weariness of walking a long path with no cheerful goal in sight, weariness and incipient fading, as well as a secret, as yet unsaid, perhaps not yet even conscious dread: fear of old age, fear of the autumn, fear of having to die. Sighing he had said farewell to her, his soul full of reluctance, and full of concealed dread.

Then Siddhartha had spent the night in his house with dancing girls and wine, he had played the superior to his peers, the superior he no longer was; he had drunk a great deal of wine and long after midnight had sought out his lair, tired and yet agitated, close to weeping and to despair, and in vain he had long sought sleep, his heart filled with misery he thought he could no longer bear, filled with revulsion, by which he felt entirely permeated, as if by the tepid, loathsome taste of the wine, by the overly sweet, desolate music, by the exceedingly soft smiles of the dancing girls, by the far-too-sweet smell of their hair and breasts. But above all else he felt disgust for himself, for his perfumed hair, the odor of wine on his breath, the tired flaccidity and the repugnance of his skin. As when one who has eaten or drunk far too much vomits it up in agony and is pleased to feel relief, so did the insomniac wish to dispose of these indulgences, these customs, this entire senseless life and himself along with it in one tremendous swell of disgust. Not until the break of day and the first waking bustle of activity on the street in front of his house in the city had he fallen asleep, for a few moments found a semi-anesthetized state, an intimation of sleep. In these moments he had a dream:

Kamala possessed a small rare songbird that she kept in a golden cage. Of this bird he dreamed. He dreamed that the bird had gone dumb, the bird which otherwise always sang at morning time, and when this struck him, he stepped up to the cage and looked inside, where the little bird lay dead and stiff at the bottom of the cage. He took the bird out, weighed him a moment in his hand and then cast him out, out into the alley, and at the very same moment he was terribly frightened, and his heart so pained him, it was as if he had cast away from himself everything of value and all things good along with the dead bird.

Suddenly awakening from this dream, he felt himself surrounded by deep melancholy. Worthless, so it seemed to him, the conduct of his life had been worthless and senseless up to that point; nothing living, nothing in any way valuable or worth keeping had remained in his hands. Alone he stood and empty, like a shipwreck on the shore.

Morose, Siddhartha retired to a pleasure garden that belonged to him, locked the gate, sat down under a mango tree, sensing death in his heart and horror in his breast, sat and sensed something dying in him, fading in him, going toward its end. Gradually he gathered his thoughts, and in his mind once again walked his life path, from the first days he could recollect. When was it that he had experienced joy, felt true rapture? O yes, several times he had experienced such things. In his boyhood he had the taste of it, when he had garnered praise from the Brahmins, having surpassed his peers, distinguishing himself in the repetition of the holy verses, in disputation with the scholars, as an assistant in the sacrifices. Then in his heart he had felt it: "A path lies before you, to which you have been called, the gods await you." And again as a young man, when the ever-elusive ever-rising goal of all contemplation had torn him from and raised him above the band of equally striving youths, when he painfully wrestled with the meaning of Brahman, when every ounce of attained knowledge only kindled new thirst in him, then again in the midst of thirst, in the midst of pain he had felt this same thing: "Onward! Onward! You have been called!" It was this voice he had heard when he had left his home and chosen the life of the shramana, and again, when he left the shramanas for that Perfect One, and also when he left him and had entered into uncertainty. How long it had been since he had heard this voice, how long since he no longer attained any heights, how level and desolate was his path past there, many long years, with no high aim, without thirst, without exaltation, content with small pleasures and yet never satisfied! All these years, without knowing it himself, he had taken pains and longed to become an ordinary human like all these many others, like these children, and in the process his life had become far more miserable and poorer than theirs, for neither their aims nor their troubles were his; this whole world of Kamaswami-people had been but a game to him, a dance that one goes to see, a comedy. Kamala alone was dear to him, had been precious to him—but was she still? Did he still need her, or she him? Did they not play a game without end? Was it necessary to live *for* the game? No, it was not necessary! The name of this game was samsara, a game for children, a game, maybe nice to play once, twice, ten times—but always and ever after?

Then Siddhartha knew that the game was at an end, that he could no longer play it. A shudder ran over his body, then it entered inside him, and so he perceived that something had died.

That entire day he sat beneath the mango tree, remembering his father, remembering Govinda, remembering Gautama. Did he have to leave these people in order to become a Kamaswami? He was still sitting there when night fell. When he looked up and gazed at the stars he thought: "Here I sit under my mango tree in my pleasure garden." He smiled a little—was it necessary, was it right, was it not a silly game, his possession of a mango tree, of a garden?

And so he was done with all this, this too died in him. He got up, bade farewell to the mango tree, bade farewell to the pleasure garden. Since he had not eaten on that day, he felt vehemently hungry, and remembered his house in the city, his chamber and bed, the table laden with food. He smiled wearily, shook himself off and bade farewell to these things.[8]

In the same hour of the night Siddhartha left his garden, left the city, never to return. For a long time Kamaswami sent people in search of him, for he believed Siddhartha had fallen into the hands of thieves. Kamala did not send anyone to search. She was not surprised to learn that Siddhartha had vanished. Had she not always expected this? Was he not a shramana, homeless, a pilgrim? And for the most part she had sensed this the last time they were together, and amidst the pain of her loss she was glad she had drawn him so intimately close to her heart, that she once more felt so entirely possessed and penetrated by him.

When she was first informed of Siddhartha's disappearance, she stepped over to the window, where she kept a rare songbird captive in a golden cage. She opened the door of the cage, took the bird out and let it fly away. For a long time she followed it with her gaze, the bird in its flight. From this day on she received no more visitors, and she kept her house locked. After some time had passed though, she was aware she was pregnant from the last time she and Siddhartha had been together.

# BY THE RIVER

Siddhartha roamed the forest, already far away from the city, with but one thought in mind, that he could no longer return, that the life he had been leading for many years was over and done, savored and sucked dry even to revulsion. Dead was the song-bird of which he had dreamed. Dead was the bird in his heart. He was deeply enmeshed in samsara, from all sides he had sucked in re-vulsion and death, as a sponge absorbs water until it is full. Glutted full, full of misery, full of death, there was nothing more in the world that could entice him, give him pleasure, bring him consolation.

Passionately he wished to know nothing more of himself, to have peace, to be dead. If only lightning would come and strike him! If only a tiger would come and devour him! If only there were a wine or a poison that would bring numbness, forgetfulness and sleep, and no more waking! Was there still some kind of filth with which he had not defiled himself, a sin or a folly he had not committed, a des-olation of the soul he had not brought upon himself? Was it still possible to live? Was it possible time and time again to inhale the breath, to exhale the breath, to feel hunger, again to eat, again to sleep, again to lie with a woman? Was this cycle not at an end for him and entirely complete?

Siddhartha arrived at the great river in the forest, at the same river across which once, when he was still a young man leaving Gau-tama's city, a ferryman had carried him. At this river he stopped and stood hesitating by the shore. Weariness and hunger had made him weak, and why should he proceed, where then, toward which desti-nation, which goal? No, there were no goals any longer, there was nothing but deep, painful yearning to shake himself free of this whole muddled dream, to spit out this stale wine, to put an end to this wretched and disgraceful life.

Over the riverbank a tree was bowed and hung, a coconut palm, Siddhartha leaned his shoulder against the trunk, wound his arm around it and gazed down into the green water that swirled and swirled below him, gazed down and found himself utterly filled with the wish to let himself go and go under in this body of water. An eerie emptiness reflected toward him out of the water, to which the terrible emptiness of his soul gave answer. Yes, he was at the end. There was nothing more for him to do but extinguish himself, to shatter this failed image of his life, to cast it at the feet of gods who laughed in scorn. This was the great emesis he had been craving: death, the shattering of the form he hated! Let the fish devour him, this dog of a Siddhartha, this lunatic, this foul and putrid body, this enervated and abused soul! Let the fishes and the crocodiles devour him, let the demons tear him apart!

Grimacing, he stared into the water, saw his face mirrored and spat at it. Utterly spent, he released his arm from the tree trunk and turned a little, so as to plummet down vertically, finally to go under. He sank, with closed eyes, down toward death.

Then from remote precincts of his soul, from the yesteryears of his exhausted life a sound vibrated. It was one word, one syllable, which without thinking he pronounced to himself in a babbling voice, the first and last word of all the old prayers of the Brahmins, the holy "*OM*," which signifies something like "the perfect" or "perfect completion." And the moment the sound "Om" touched Siddhartha's ear, his slumbering mind awakened and recognized the folly of his action.

Siddhartha was deeply shocked. So it had come to this: so lost was he, so far astray and abandoned by all knowledge that he could seek death, that this wish, this childish wish could mature in him: to find peace by extinguishing his body! What all the torment of these recent times, all the disillusionment, all the despair had not effected, the very moment the Om penetrated his consciousness had: he recognized himself in his misery and in his error.[9]

Om! he said to himself: Om! And he knew of Brahman, knew of

the indestructibility of life, knew again of everything divine, which he had forgotten.

Yet this was only a moment, a flash. At the foot of the coconut palm Siddhartha sank down, exhausted, prone, mumbling Om, he set his head on the tree root and sank into a deep sleep.

Deep was his sleep and dreamless, he had not known such a sleep for a long time. When he awakened after many hours, to him it was as if ten years had gone by, he heard the gentle rushing of the water, did not know where he was or who had brought him to this place, opened his eyes, saw with astonishment trees and sky above him, and remembered where he was and how he had come here. Still, for this he needed a long while, and the past seemed covered by a veil, infinitely remote, infinitely distant, infinitely indifferent. He knew only that his former life (in the first moment of consciousness this former life appeared to him like a long-gone, prior incarnation, like an early pre-birth of his present I)—that he had left his former life, that full of revulsion and misery he had even wanted to dispose of his life, but that by a river, under a coconut palm, he came to himself, the holy word Om on his lips, then he had fallen asleep, and now awake he looked into the world as a new man. Softly he spoke the word Om to himself, as he had done while falling asleep, and it seemed to him as if his whole long sleep had been nothing but a long, rapt recitation of Om, a meditation on Om, an immersion and complete entrance into the Om, into the nameless, the perfect.

What a wondrous sleep this had been after all! Never had sleep so refreshed him, so renewed him, so rejuvenated him! Maybe he really had died, had perished and been reborn in a new form? But no, he knew himself, he knew his own hands and his feet, knew the place where he lay, knew this I in his breast, this Siddhartha, willful, peculiar, but this Siddhartha nonetheless was transformed, was refreshed, was remarkably well rested, remarkably awake, joyful and inquisitive.

Siddhartha sat up straight when he saw, seated across from him in the posture of meditation, a person, a strange man, a monk in a yellow robe with a shaved head. He looked closely at the man, who had no hair on his head or face, and it was not long before he recognized Govinda in the monk, Govinda, the friend of his youth, who had taken refuge in the exalted Buddha. Govinda had grown old, he as well, but his face still bore its old features, and it spoke of diligence, of faithfulness, of seeking, of timidity. But now as Govinda felt his gaze, opened his eyes and looked at him, Siddhartha saw that Govinda did not recognize him. Govinda was happy to find him awake, apparently he had been sitting here a long time and waiting for him to awaken, even though he did not know him.

"I have been sleeping," Siddhartha said. "How is it that you have come here?"

"You have been sleeping," Govinda answered. "It is not good to sleep in such places, where snakes and wild animals often have their trails. I, good Sir, am a disciple of the exalted Gautama, of the Buddha, of Shakyamuni, and a number of us were making a pilgrimage on this road, when I saw you lying here and sleeping in a place where it is dangerous to sleep. For that reason I tried to awaken you, good Sir, and when I saw that your sleep was very deep, I remained here behind my brothers and sat with you. And then, so it seems, I myself fell asleep, I who wanted to watch over your sleep. I have performed my duty badly; weariness overcame me. But now, since you are awake, allow me to go so that I may catch up with my brothers."

"I thank you, Shramana, for having protected my sleep," Siddhartha said. "Friendly are the disciples of the Exalted One. Now you may go."

"I am going, Sir. May the gentleman always find himself well."

"I thank you, Shramana."

Govinda gave him a sign of salutation and said: "Farewell."

"Farewell, Govinda," Siddhartha replied.

The monk stopped where he was standing.

"Excuse me, Sir, however do you know my name?"

Then Siddhartha smiled.

"I know you, o Govinda, from your father's hut, and from the school for Brahmins, and from the offerings, and from our time with the shramanas, and from that hour when in the grove, in the Jetavana you took your refuge in the Exalted One."

"You are Siddhartha!" Govinda exclaimed loudly. "Now I recognize you and no longer grasp how I could fail to do so immediately. Welcome, Siddhartha, I feel great joy seeing you again."

"It gladdens me too to see you again. You have been the watchman of my sleep, again I thank you for that, although I did not require a watchman. Where are you going, my Friend?"

"Nowhere is where I'm going. We monks are always underway, as long as it is not the rainy season, we always move from place to place, living according to the precepts, announcing the teachings, collecting alms, moving on. It is always so. But you, Siddhartha, where are you going?"

Siddhartha spoke: "It is the same with me, Friend, as with you. I am not going anywhere. I am just underway. I am on a pilgrimage."

Govinda spoke: "You say you are on a pilgrimage, and I believe you. But pardon, o Siddhartha, you do not resemble a pilgrim. You wear the garb of a rich man, you wear the shoes of a nobleman, and your hair, scented with perfumed water, is not the hair of a pilgrim, not the hair of a shramana."

"Well, dear Friend, you have observed well, your sharp eye sees all. But I did not say to you I am a shramana. I said: I am on a pilgrimage. And so it is: I am on a pilgrimage."

"You are on a pilgrimage," Govinda stated. "But few go on a pilgrimage in such clothing, few in such shoes, few with such hair. Never have I, who for many years have been on a pilgrimage, met such a pilgrim."

"I believe you, my dear Govinda. But now, today for the first time, you have just met one such pilgrim, in such shoes, in such attire. Remember, my dear: Transient is the world of forms, transient, highly transient are our clothing and the ways in which we dress our hair, just as our hair and our bodies themselves. I wear the clothes of a rich man, that you have seen correctly. I wear them because I have

been a rich man, and wear my hair like men of the world and volup-
tuaries, because I have been one of them."

"And now, Siddhartha, what are you now?"

"I do not know, I know as little as you. I am underway. I was a rich
man, and no longer am; and what I shall be tomorrow I do not
know."

"You have lost your riches?"

"I have lost my riches, or they me. They are out of my hands. The
wheel of forms turns quickly, Govinda. Where is Siddhartha the
Brahmin? Where is Siddhartha the shramana? Where is Siddhartha
the rich man? Quickly the mutable changes, Govinda, you know
that."

Govinda gazed long at the friend of his youth, with doubt in his
eyes. Then he saluted him as one salutes a member of the nobility,
and he went his way.

With a smile on his face Siddhartha looked back at him, loving
this faithful and timid man as he always had. And why—at this moment, this glorious hour after his marvelous sleep, permeated by
Om—should he not have loved someone or something! The enchantment that had occurred in sleep and through the Om consisted
in just that: he loved everything, he was filled with joyful love for all
he saw. And it seemed to him now this was exactly why he had been
so terribly sick before: he had been incapable of loving anything or
anyone.

With a smile on his face Siddhartha looked back at the monks who
were walking away. Sleep had made him much stronger, but hunger
was a great torment, for now he had gone two days without eating,
and a long time had passed since he had hardened himself against
hunger. With distress and yet with laughter too he remembered that
time. Back then, so he recalled, he boasted of three things to Kamala,
he had mastered three noble and insuperable arts: fasting—waiting—
thinking. This was all he possessed, his power and strength, his
steady staff, in the diligent, painstaking years of his youth he had
learned these three arts, nothing else. And now they had deserted

him, none of them was his any longer, not fasting, not waiting, not thinking. He had sacrificed them for what was most miserable, what was most fleeting, for sensuality, for a life of luxury, for riches! Strange things really did happen to him. And now, so it seemed, now he really had become one of the child people.

Siddhartha brooded over his situation a long time. Thinking did not come easily to him, basically he had no desire to, nonetheless he forced himself.

Now, he thought, as all these most fleeting things have slipped away from me again, now again I stand under the sun, as I once did as a child, nothing is mine, I know nothing, I can do nothing, I have learned nothing. How strange this is! Now, no longer young, my hair already half gray, my powers failing, now I begin again at the beginning as a child! Again he had to smile. Yes, his fate was odd. Things went downhill for him, and again he stood naked in the world, vacant and slow. But he felt no regret over it, in fact, he felt a great impulse to laugh, to laugh at himself, to laugh at this strange, foolish world.

"Things are going downhill for you!" he said to himself and laughed, and while saying this, his gaze fell upon the river, and he saw the river too was tumbling down, always rambling downward, and yet it was singing and happy at the same time. This pleased him greatly, he gave a friendly smile to the river. Was this not the river in which he had wished to drown, once, a hundred years ago, or had it been a dream?

Strange indeed my life has been, he thought to himself, it has taken strange roundabout routes. As a boy I was concerned only with gods and sacrifices. As a youth I was concerned only with asceticism, with thinking and meditation; I was searching for Brahman, venerated the eternal in Atman. As a young man though I followed the penitents, lived in the forest, suffered heat and frost, learned to go hungry, instructed my body to feel nothing. Miraculously then the teachings of the great Buddha were revealed to me, I felt knowledge of the unity of the world circulate in me like my own blood. But even from Buddha and from the great knowledge I had to walk on again. I went and learned the pleasures of love from Kamala, learned business from Kamaswami, made piles of money, lost money, learned to love my stomach, learned to cater to my senses. It took me many years to lose the power of my intellect, to unlearn how to think, to forget the unity. Is it not the case, does it not seem as if I have slowly and on long roundabout routes gone from manhood to childhood, gone from being a thinker to a child person? And yet this path has been very good, and yet the bird in my breast has not died. But what a path it has been! I have had to endure so much stupidity, so many burdens, so much error, so much disgust and disappointment and misery simply to become a child again and to be able to begin fresh. But it was rightly so, my heart affirms it, my eyes laugh at it. I had to experience despair, I had to sink down to the most misguided of all thoughts, to the thought of suicide, in order to experience grace, again to perceive Om, again to sleep well and properly to awaken. I had to become a fool in order again to find Atman within myself. I had to sin to be able to live again. Where else may my path still lead me? Ridiculous is this path, it loops around, it may even go in circles. May it go where it will, wherever it goes I will follow.

Wonderful, the joy he felt welling up in his breast.

From where then, he asked his heart, where have you found this mirth? Has it come from the long, good sleep that has done me so much good? Or from the word Om I pronounced? Or from my having escaped, that my flight is over, that I am finally free again and like a child I stand under the open sky? O how good it is to have fled, to have become free! How pure and beautiful the air is here, how good it is to breathe! There, where I ran away from, everything reeked of salves, of spices, of wine, of boredom, of indolence. How I hated this world of the rich, of gluttons, of gamblers! How I hated myself, remaining so long in that frightful world! How I hated myself, robbed myself, poisoned, tormented, making myself old and evil! No, no longer will I, as I once so gladly did, delude myself that Siddhartha is wise! I have made up for this, however, and this pleases me, this I must praise: this self-hatred has now come to an end, this foolish and muddled life is over! I commend you, Siddhartha, after so many years of folly, once again you have had an insight, you have done something, you have heard the bird singing in your breast and have followed it!

So he praised himself, was delighted with himself, listened with curiosity to his stomach that growled with hunger. Now he felt that in recent days and times he had utterly chewed his way through one portion of woe and another of misery, tasting and spitting them out, devouring them even unto despair, even unto death. And that this was good. He could long have remained with Kamaswami, acquiring money, squandering money, fattening his belly and allowing his soul to die of thirst, he could long have resided in this soft, well-upholstered hell, had this not occurred: the moment of complete inconsolability and despair, that most extreme moment when he perched above the rushing water, ready to annihilate himself. He had felt despair and deepest revulsion, and he had not succumbed; the bird, the fresh wellspring and voice was still alive within him; this made him feel joy, this is why he laughed, this is why beneath his gray hair his face was radiant.

"It is good," he thought, "oneself to sample everything one needs to know. That worldly pleasure and riches are not good I already learned as a child. For a long time I knew it, but I have experienced it only now. And now I know it, know it not only by heart, but also *with* my heart, with my eyes, with my stomach. Good for me, that I know it!"

For a long time he reflected over his transformation, listened to the bird, how it sang for joy. Had this bird not died inside him, had he not felt it die? No, something else had died in him, something that had long been yearning to die. Was it not this thing that once, in his glowing-hot years as a penitent, he had wanted to kill off? Was it not his I, his small, proud and fearful I, with which he had fought for so many years, which had always conquered him, which always remained after every annihilation, forbidding joy, sensing fear? Was it not this, which today finally had met its death, here in the forest by this lovely river? Was it not because of this death that he now was like a child, so full of trust, so fearless, so full of joy?

Now too Siddhartha surmised why he as a Brahmin, as a penitent had fought in vain with this I. Too much knowledge had hindered him, too many holy verses, too many rules concerning sacrifices, too much castigation, too much doing and striving! He had been full of arrogance, always the cleverest, always the most diligent, always one step ahead of all the others, always the knowledgeable one, the intellectual, always the priest or the wise man. Into this priesthood, into this arrogance, into this intellectuality his I had crept in and holed up, it sat there and grew, while he meant to kill it with fasting and repentance. Now he saw it, and saw that the secret voice had been right, that no teacher yet had been able to save him. That is why he had to go out into the world, lose himself in pleasure and power, in women and money, he had to become a merchant, a dice player, a drinker and a greedy man, until the priest and shramana in him were dead. That is why he had to endure those hideous years, bear the disgust, the instruction, the senselessness of a barren and irrecoverable life, even to the end, even to bitter despair, even until the voluptuary Siddhartha, the avaricious Siddhartha could die. He was dead, a new Siddhartha had awakened from sleep. He too would grow old, he too one day would have to die, transitory was Siddhartha, transitory was every form. But today he was young, the new Siddhartha was a child, and he was full of joy.[10]

These were the thoughts he thought, listening to his stomach with a smile, thankfully listening to the buzzing of a single bee. Blithely he gazed into the flowing river, never had a body of water pleased him as much as this, never had he heard the voice and likeness of this current of water so strong and beautiful. It seemed that the water had something special to say to him, something he still did not know, that still awaited him. In this river Siddhartha had wanted to drown himself; in it the old, tired, despairing Siddhartha today was drowned. The new Siddhartha, however, felt a deep love for this flowing water, and himself resolved not to leave it again so soon.

# THE FERRYMAN

By this river I want to remain, Siddhartha thought, the same one I came to when I was on my way to the child people, back then a friendly ferryman took me across, to him I want to go, from outside his hut my path once led to a new life, which has now grown old and died—may my current path, my current new life issue from there also!

Fondly he gazed into the rushing water, into the transparent green, into the crystalline lines of its mysterious design. He saw bright pearls rising up from the depths, tranquil air bubbles swimming to the reflective surface, imaging the blue of the sky. With a thousand eyes the river gazed at him, with green, with white, with crystalline, with azure eyes. How he loved this water, how it enchanted him, how grateful he was to it! In his heart he heard the voice speaking, the newly awakened voice, and it said to him: Love this water! Stay here! Learn from it! O yes, he wanted to learn from the water, he wanted to listen to it. Whoever understood this water and its secrets, it seemed to him, that person would understand much else, many secrets, all secrets.

Of the river's secrets, however, today he saw only one that seized his soul: This water ran on and on, it always ran, and yet it always was there, it was always and ever the same and yet at every moment new! Lucky the man who grasped this, who understood this! He did not understand or grasp it, he only sensed the stirring of a surmise, a distant memory, divine voices.

Siddhartha rose, the pressure of hunger in his body became unbearable. Tolerating it, he walked on, following the path along the bank, upstream, listening to the flow, listening to the growling hunger in his body.

When he reached the ferry, the boat lay ready, and the same ferryman who once had carried the young shramana across the river stood in the boat; Siddhartha recognized him again, he too had aged greatly.

"Will you conduct me across?" he asked.

The ferryman, astonished to see such an elegant man alone and on foot, took him into the boat and pushed off.

"What a beautiful life you have chosen for yourself," said the passenger. "How lovely it must be to live by the water every day and to travel on it."

Smiling, the oarsman rocked as he rowed: "It is lovely, Sir, it is as you say. But is not every life, is not every kind of work lovely?"

"It may well be. But it is you and yours that I envy."

"Oh, you would soon lose your relish in it. It is not for people in fine clothes."

Siddhartha laughed. "Already once today I was regarded with distrust on account of my clothing. Ferryman, will you not accept these clothes from me, which have become a burden? For I must inform you that I have no money with which to pay the fare."

"The gentleman speaks in jest," the ferryman laughed.

"I am not joking, Friend. You see, once before you took me across this water in your boat for god's reward. Do so again today, and accept my clothing in recompense."

"And does the gentleman wish to travel onward without clothing?"

"Oh, what I would most like to do is put an end to my travels. Ferryman, it would suit me best if you would give me an old apron and keep me with you as your assistant, or rather as your apprentice, because first I need to learn how to handle the boat."

For a long time the ferryman looked searchingly at the stranger.

"Now I recognize you," he said at last. "Once you slept in my hut, it was long ago, maybe more than twenty years, and you were brought across the river by me, and we parted as good friends. Were you not a shramana? I can no longer recall your name."

"My name is Siddhartha, and I was a shramana, when you last saw me."

"Welcome, then, Siddhartha. My name is Vasudeva.[11] I hope you will be my guest again today, and that you will sleep in my hut, and tell me where you come from, and why your lovely clothes have become a burden to you."

They had reached the middle of the river and Vasudeva pulled the oars more strongly, in order to make way against the current. Calmly he worked, with sinewy arms, his gaze fixed on the prow of the boat. Siddhartha sat and looked at him, and remembered how back on the final day of his time as a shramana, love for this man had stirred his heart. Gratefully he accepted Vasudeva's invitation. When they landed on the opposite shore, he helped him tie the boat to the posts, after which the ferryman invited him into his hut, offered him bread and water, and Siddhartha ate with pleasure, eating with pleasure too of the mangos Vasudeva offered him.

Afterward they sat down—it was getting toward sunset—on a tree bole by the riverbank, and Siddhartha told the ferryman of his parentage and his life, and how it had appeared to his eyes today, in his hour of despair. His storytelling went on deep into the night.

Vasudeva listened with great attentiveness. He took everything in as he listened, Siddhartha's ancestry and childhood, all the learning, all the seeking, all the joys, all the misery. Among all the ferryman's virtues this was one of the greatest: he understood how to listen as very few did. Vasudeva spoke not a word himself, and yet the speaker sensed how he allowed the speaker's words to enter him, with tranquility, openly, waiting, how he lost not a one, waiting without impatience, without praise or blame, simply listening. Siddhartha felt what a joy it is to tell everything, to sink one's own life, one's own seeking, one's own suffering into such a listener's heart.

Toward the end of Siddhartha's tale, however, when he told of the tree over the river, and of his deep fall, of the sacred Om, and how he had felt such great love for the river after his slumber, then the ferryman listened with doubled attention, entirely and completely captivated, with closed eyes.

But as Siddhartha fell silent, and the silence held a long time, Vasudeva spoke: "It is as I thought. The river has spoken to you. It is your friend as well, it speaks to you, too. This is good, this is very good. Stay with me, Siddhartha, my friend. Once I had a wife, her bed was beside mine, but she died a long time ago, I have lived alone for a long time. Live with me now, there is room enough and food enough for us both."

"I thank you," Siddhartha replied, "I thank you and I accept. And I also thank you, Vasudeva, for having listened so well to me! Rare are those people who understand how to listen, and I have met no one who understands as you do. In this, too, I will learn from you."

"You will learn how," Vasudeva said, "but not from me. The river taught me how to listen, from the river you too will learn how. It knows everything, the river, one can learn everything from it. Look here, from the water you have already learned it is good to strive for the bottom, to sink, to seek out the depths. The wealthy and elegant Siddhartha will be a galley slave, the learned Brahmin Siddhartha will become a ferryman: this too the river has told you. You will also learn the other thing from it."

Siddhartha spoke after a long pause, "What other thing, Vasudeva?"

Vasudeva rose. "It has gotten late," he said, "let us go to sleep. I cannot say what 'other thing,' o Friend. You will learn it, perhaps you already know it. Look here, I am no scholar, I do not understand how to speak, I do not understand how to think either. I understand only how to listen and be pious, I have learned nothing else. If I could speak and teach, maybe then I would be a sage, but I am only a ferryman, and my task is to take people across the river. Many have I transported, thousands, and for all of them my river has been nothing but an obstacle on their journeys. They traveled for money and business, and to weddings and on pilgrimages, and the river was in their way, and then the ferryman was there, to get them quickly over their obstacle. For some few among the thousands, however, a very few, four or five, the river stopped being a hindrance, they had heard its voice, they listened to it, and the river has become holy to them, as it has become to me. Let us now take our rest, Siddhartha."

Siddhartha remained with the ferryman and learned to handle the boat, and when not occupied with the ferry, he worked with Vasudeva in the rice paddy, gathered wood, plucked the fruits of the plantain trees. He learned how to make an oar, how to repair the boat, how to weave baskets, and he was cheerful about everything he learned, and the days and months passed quickly. More though than Vasudeva could teach him, the river taught him. From it he learned ceaselessly. Above all he learned how to listen, to hearken with a quiet heart, with a soul that waited, open, without passion, without desire, without judgment, without opinion.

He lived in friendship beside Vasudeva, and sometimes they would exchange words with each other, few and well-considered words. Vasudeva was no friend of words, Siddhartha seldom succeeded in inducing him to speak.

"Have you," he asked once, "have you also learned this secret from the river: that time does not exist?"

A bright smile spread over Vasudeva's face.

"Yes, Siddhartha," he said. "But do you not mean that the river is everywhere at once, at its origin and at its mouth, at the waterfall, at the ferry, at the rapids, in the sea, in the mountains, everywhere at the same time, and for it only the present exists, no shadow of the past, no shadow of the future?"

"That is it," said Siddhartha. "And when I learned that, I took a look at my life and saw that it too was a river, and the boy Siddhartha was separated from the man Siddhartha and from the graybeard Siddhartha only by shadows, not by anything real. And there was no past for Siddhartha's earlier births, and his death and his return to Brahma are without future. Nothing was, nothing will be; everything is, everything has essence, is present."[12]

Siddhartha spoke as one enraptured, this enlightenment brought him deep bliss. O, was not all suffering time, all self-torment and self-fear—time? All the world's difficulty, all the world's animosity, would they not be gone and conquered, once time was conquered, once it could be thought away? Enraptured he had spoken; Vasudeva, however, smiled radiantly at him and nodded in affirmation; silently he nodded, ran his hand over Siddhartha's shoulder, and turned back to his work.

And once again, during the rainy season even as the river was swollen and roared mightily, Siddhartha spoke: "Is it not true, o Friend, the river has many voices, very many voices? Has it not the voice of a king, and of a warrior, and of a bull, and of a nightbird, and of a woman giving birth, and of someone sighing, and still a thousand other voices?"

"That is so," Vasudeva nodded, "all the voices of creation are in its voice."

"And do you know," Siddhartha continued, "which word it speaks, when you succeed in hearing all its ten thousand voices at the same time?"

Vasudeva's face laughed happily, he bent toward Siddhartha and spoke the holy Om into his ear. And this was just what Siddhartha, too, had heard.

And over time his smile became more and more like that of the ferryman, it grew almost as radiant, it glowed nearly as blissfully, equally luminous out of the thousand little folds, equally childlike, equally senile. Many travelers, if they saw both ferrymen, took them for brothers. Often in the evening they sat down on the bole of the tree by the riverbank, both holding silent and listening to the water, which for them was no body of water, but rather the voice of life, the voice of being, of eternal becoming. And sometimes it happened that both, while listening to the river, thought of the same things, of a conversation from the day before yesterday, of one of their passengers, whose face and fate occupied them, of death, of their childhood, and if the river had said something good to them, both in the same moment would look at each other, both with exactly the same thought, both delighted with the same answer to the same question.

Something emanated from the ferry and the two ferrymen which many a traveler felt. It sometimes happened that a traveler, after having looked into the face of one of the ferrymen, began to tell the story of his life, told all his troubles, confessed his bad deeds, asking for consolation and advice. It sometimes happened that one of them asked permission to spend an evening with them to listen to the river. It also happened that inquisitive people came, who had heard that two wise men or magicians or saints lived by this ferry. The inquisitive people asked many questions but received no answers, and they found neither sorcerers nor sages; all they found were two friendly little old men, who seemed mute and a bit odd and somewhat gaga. And the inquiring people laughed, and discussed how foolhardy and gullible people who spread such empty rumors were.

The years went by and no one counted them. Then one day monks came on a pilgrimage, adherents of the Gautama, of the Buddha, who asked to be taken across the river, and from them the ferrymen learned that they were hurriedly returning to their great teacher, because the news had spread, the Exalted One was deathly ill and soon would die his final human death, in order to be released. It was not long before there came a new troop of monks, and again another, and the monks as well as most of the other travelers and people on foot spoke of nothing but Gautama and his approaching death. And just as people come streaming from everywhere and from all sides to a military expedition or to the coronation of a king, themselves banding together like an army of ants, so they streamed, as if drawn by a magic spell, to where the great Buddha awaited his death, where something unheard-of would take place and the supreme Perfect One of an era would pass into glory.

At this time Siddhartha remembered a lot about the dying sage, the great teacher, whose voice had exhorted nations and awakened hundreds of thousands, whose voice he too once had heard, whose holy countenance he too once had beheld with reverence. Benignly he remembered him, saw his path of perfection before his eyes, and remembered with a smile the words he once as a young man had leveled at the Exalted One. Proud and precocious words they had been, it now seemed, he smiled to recall them. For some time he knew he was no longer separated from Gautama, whose teachings he had nonetheless been unable to accept. No, a true seeker could accept no teachings, not one who truly desired to find. But one who had found, he was capable of approving every teaching, every path, every goal, nothing separated him any longer from all the thousands of others who lived in eternity, who breathed the divine.

On one of these days, when so many were making pilgrimage to the dying Buddha, Kamala, once the most beautiful of all the courtesans, was also on a pilgrimage to him. Long ago she had withdrawn from her previous life, giving her garden to Gautama's monks, taking her refuge in the teachings, she was among the friends and patronesses of the pilgrims. Together with the boy Siddhartha, her son, upon hearing the news of the approaching death of Gautama, she had taken to the road, simply dressed, on foot. She was on the road by the river with her young son; the boy, however, soon grew tired, wanted to go home, wanted to rest, wanted to eat, became stubborn, whined. Kamala frequently had to rest with him, he was accustomed to asserting his will against her, she had to feed him, console him, scold him. He did not understand why he had to go on this arduous and cheerless pilgrimage with his mother, to an unknown place, to a strange man who was holy and lay dying. Let him die, what did this have to do with the boy?

The pilgrims were no longer far from Vasudeva's ferry when the little Siddhartha again forced his mother to rest. Even she herself, Kamala, was exhausted, and while the boy was chewing on a banana, she crouched down on the ground, closed her eyes some, and rested. But suddenly she uttered a cry of lamentation, the boy looked at her in shock and saw her face blanch with horror, and a small black adder, which had bitten Kamala, escaped from under her dress.

Now the two of them ran quickly on the path in search of people, and they came near to the ferry, where Kamala collapsed, and could go no farther. The boy, however, raised a piteous hue and cry, all the while kissing his mother and hanging on her neck, and her voice joined in his loud cries for help, until the tones reached Vasudeva's ear, as he stood by the ferry. Quickly he came, took the woman into his arms, carried her to the boat, the boy ran alongside and soon they all arrived in the hut, where Siddhartha stood at the hearth, lighting a fire. He looked up and first saw the face of the boy, which was a strange reminder, admonishing him of something forgotten. Then he saw Kamala, whom he instantly recognized, although she lay unconscious in the arms of the ferryman, and now he knew that this was his own son whose face had admonished him so strongly, and his heart moved in his breast.

Kamala's wound was washed, but it was already black and her body was swollen; a healing infusion was prepared for her. Her consciousness returned, she lay on Siddhartha's bed in the hut, and Siddhartha bent over her, he who had once loved her so much. To her it seemed a dream, smiling she looked into her friend's face, only slowly did she become aware of her situation, remembering the bite, crying out in anguish for the boy.

"He is here with you, do not be alarmed," Siddhartha said.

Kamala looked into his eyes. She spoke with a heavy tongue, paralyzed by the poison. "You have grown old, my love," she said, "you have grown gray. But you resemble the young shramana who once came to me in the garden, without clothing, your feet covered with dust. You resemble him far more now than you did at the time you left me and Kamaswami. In your eyes you are like him, Siddhartha. Oh, I too have grown old, old—and yet you still recognized me?"

Siddhartha smiled: "I knew you at once, Kamala, my love."

Kamala pointed to her boy and said: "Did you recognize him too? He is your son."

Her eyes strayed wildly and fell closed. The boy cried; Siddhartha took him onto his lap, let him cry, stroked his hair, and the sight of the child's face recalled to him a Brahminic prayer, one he himself had learned as a little boy. Slowly, in a singsong, he began to chant, out of his past, his childhood, the words came pouring. And during his chanting the child calmed down, sobbed now and again and fell asleep. Siddhartha lay him on Vasudeva's bed. Vasudeva stood at the hearth cooking rice. Siddhartha cast a glance in his direction, which he returned with a smile.

"She will die," Siddhartha said gently.

Vasudeva nodded, the firelight from the hearth spread over his friendly face.

Once again Kamala regained consciousness. Pain disfigured her face, Siddhartha's eyes read the suffering in her mouth, on her cheeks that had turned pale. Quietly he read it, attentive, waiting, sunk in her suffering. Kamala felt this, her gaze sought his.

Looking at him, she said: "Now I see that your eyes, too, have changed. They are entirely different. How then do I still know you are Siddhartha? You are and you are not the same."

Siddhartha did not speak, his eyes looked tranquilly into hers.

"You have attained it?" she asked. "You have found peace?"

He smiled and laid his hand upon hers.

"I can see it," she said, "I see it. I too shall find peace."

"You have found it," Siddhartha spoke in a whisper.

Kamala looked him unwaveringly in the eye. She remembered wanting to make a pilgrimage to Gautama in order to see the face of the one perfect man, to inhale his peace, but that instead of him, now she had found Siddhartha, and it was good, just as good, as having seen the other. She wanted to tell him this, but her tongue no longer obeyed her will. Holding silence, she looked at him, and he saw the life go out in her eyes. As the final pain filled her gaze and clouded it, and as the last shudder ran through her limbs, his finger closed her eyelids.

For a long time he sat and looked at her face now lost in sleep. For a long time he gazed upon her mouth, the tired old mouth with narrowed lips, and he remembered that once, in his life's springtime, he had compared this mouth to a fig freshly split open. For a long time he sat reading the pale face, the tired creases, filling himself with the sight, he saw his own face lying like that, just as white, just as extinguished, and at once saw his face and hers—young, with red lips, with burning eyes, and the feeling of the present and simultaneity completely pervaded him, the feeling of eternity. Deeply, more deeply than ever, in this hour he sensed the indestructibility of every life, the eternity of every moment.

When he got up, Vasudeva had prepared rice for him. Yet Siddhartha ate nothing. In the barn, with their goat, the two old men made a bed of straw, and Vasudeva lay down to sleep. But Siddhartha went out and sat all night before the hut, listening to the river, like a rock in the stream of the past, touched and surrounded by all the times of his life at once. Sometimes though he got up, walked to the door of the hut and listened to hear whether the boy was sleeping.

Early in the morning, still before the sun was visible, Vasudeva came out of the barn and walked over to his friend.

"You have not slept," he said.

"No, Vasudeva. I sat here, I listened to the river. It told me a great deal, it filled me deeply with healing thoughts, with thoughts of unity."

"You have suffered pain, Siddhartha, yet I see, no sadness has entered your heart."

"No, my dear, why then should I be sad? I, the I who was rich and happy have now become even richer and happier. My son has been given to me."

"Your son is welcome here with me as well. But now, Siddhartha, let us get to work, there is much to do. Kamala has died on the same bed my wife once died upon. On the same hill too we shall build Kamala's funeral pyre, the one on which I once built my wife's funeral pyre."

While the boy still slept, they built the funeral pyre.[13]

# THE SON

Shy and weeping, the boy had witnessed his mother's burial;
dark and shy he had listened to Siddhartha, who greeted him
as his son and welcomed him to live with them in Vasudeva's
hut. All day long he sat on the hill of the dead, pale, not wanting to
eat, keeping his eyes shut, locking up his heart, bristling against fate,
resisting it.

Siddhartha spared him and let him be, honoring his grief. Siddhartha understood that his son did not know him, that he could
not love him like a father. Slowly he saw and also understood that
this eleven-year-old was a spoiled child, a mother's boy who had
grown up accustomed to wealth, accustomed to fine cooking, a soft
bed, accustomed to ordering servants around. Siddhartha understood that this mourner, this spoiled child could not suddenly and
graciously acquiesce to a life of poverty in a place that was strange to
him. He did not force him, he did many chores for him, always
culling the choicest morsels for the boy. He hoped slowly to win him
over, through benign patience.

He had called himself rich and fortunate when the boy had come
to him. But as time flowed on, and the boy remained alien and
gloomy, exhibiting a proud and stubborn heart, disdaining to work,
showing no respect for his elders, stealing from Vasudeva's fruit
trees, Siddhartha gradually understood this was not good fortune
and peace that had come to him with the boy, rather pain and sorrow. He loved him nonetheless, preferring love's pain and sorrow to
good fortune and joy without him.

Since the young Siddhartha had come to live in the hut, the old
men had divided their labors. Vasudeva had taken over the ferryman's post alone once again and Siddhartha, in order to be with his
son, worked in the hut and the field.

For a long time, for long months Siddhartha waited for his son to understand him, to accept his love, perhaps to return it. For long months Vasudeva waited, witnessing, he waited and kept silent. One day, when the young Siddhartha wore on his father's nerves with spitefulness and moodiness and again had broken both rice bowls, that evening Vasudeva took his friend aside and spoke to him.

"Excuse me," he said, "I speak from my heart and out of friendship. I see you are tormenting yourself, I see your affliction. Your son, dear friend, troubles you, and he troubles me as well. The young bird is accustomed to a different life, a different nest. Unlike you, he has not run from riches and the city out of revulsion and glut, he had to leave all that behind against his will. I asked the river, o Friend, I have asked it many times. But the river laughs, it laughs at me, it laughs at you and me both, it rattles with laughter at our foolishness. Water chooses water, youth chooses youth, your son is not in a place where he can thrive. Go and ask the river too, go and listen to what it tells you!"

Distressed, Siddhartha gazed into his friendly face, in whose many wrinkles cheerfulness perennially dwelled.

"Can I part from him then?" he asked softly, ashamed. "Give me time, dear friend! Look, I am fighting for him, I am competing for his heart, with love and with kindly patience I will capture it. The river will speak to him one day as well, he too is called."

Vasudeva's smile bloomed more warmly. "O yes, he too is called, he too is of life eternal. But do we know then, you and I, to what he is called, to which path, to which deeds, to which suffering? His suffering will not be small, proud and hard is his heart, people like him will suffer much, stray much, do much wrong, saddle themselves with much transgression. Tell me, dear friend: how do you rear your son? Do you not force him to do anything? Do you not strike him? Do you not administer punishment?"

"No, Vasudeva, I do none of those things."

"I knew that. You do not coerce him, you do not strike him, you do not give him orders, for you know that soft is stronger than hard, water stronger than rock, love stronger than force. Very good, I praise you. But do you not err in supposing that you are not coercing him, that you are not punishing him? Does your love not bind him with bands? Do you not shame him every day, making it even more difficult for him with your benevolence and your patience? Are you not forcing an arrogant and spoiled boy to live in a hut with two old banana-eaters, for whom rice is a delicacy, whose thoughts cannot be his, whose hearts are old and quiet and beat differently from his? Is not all this coercion and punishment to him?"

Stricken, Siddhartha gazed down at the ground. Softly he asked: "What do you think I should do?"

Vasudeva spoke: "Bring him to the city, bring him to his mother's house; there should still be servants there, give him to them. And if no one is there any longer, bring him to a teacher, not for the sake of instruction, but so that he will come into contact with other boys, and with girls, and come into the world that is his own. Have you never considered this?"

"You see into my heart," Siddhartha said with sadness. "Often I have thought about this. But look, how can I give him, who moreover has no softness in his heart, how can I give him to this world? Will he not become pompous, will he not lose himself in pleasure and power, will he not repeat all his father's mistakes, will he not perhaps entirely lose himself in samsara?"

The ferryman's smile beamed brightly; he gently touched Siddhartha's arm and said, "Ask the river about it, Friend! Hear it laugh out loud! Do you really believe you have committed your follies so that your son may be spared them? And that you can save your son from samsara? How? Through instruction, through prayer, through exhortation? Dear friend, have you completely forgotten the tale, the highly instructive tale of Siddhartha, the Brahmin's son, that you once told me here on this very spot? Who preserved Siddhartha the shramana from samsara, from sin, from avarice, from folly? Did his father's piety, his teachers' exhortations, could his own knowledge, his own seeking preserve him? Which father, which teacher could shield him from living his own life, dirtying his own hands with life, saddling himself with guilt, himself drinking the bitter drink, himself finding his path? Do you believe, dear friend, that perhaps anyone at all is spared this path? Maybe your little son, because you love him, because you would like to spare him suffering and pain and disappointment? But even if you were to die ten deaths for him, you still would be unable to diminish the smallest part of his fate for him."

Never before had Vasudeva spoken so many words. Siddhartha thanked him kindly, went into the hut in anguish, for a long time found no sleep. Vasudeva had said nothing he himself had not thought and known. But it was a knowledge he could do nothing about, stronger than this knowledge was his love for the boy, stronger his affection, his fear of losing him. Had he ever lost his heart so deeply to anything at all, had he ever loved a human being so much, so blindly, with such intense pain, so fruitlessly, and yet so happily?

Siddhartha could not follow his friend's advice, he could not give his son away. He let the boy order him around, he let the boy disobey him. He kept silence and waited, daily he began the mute battle of congeniality, the soundless warfare of patience. Vasudeva also kept silence and waited, amiably, knowing, long-suffering. Of patience they were both masters.

Once, when the boy's face greatly reminded him of Kamala, Siddhartha suddenly was forced to recall something Kamala had said to him once in days gone by, in the days of their youth. "You cannot love," she had said to him, and he told her she was right and had compared himself with a star; the child people, however, he compared with falling leaves, and yet he had also felt a reproach in her words. Indeed he never had been able to lose himself entirely, to give himself entirely to another person, to forget himself, to commit follies of love on account of another; never had he been able to do this, and it seemed to him back then that this was the great divide separating him from the child people. But now, ever since his son was there, now even he, Siddhartha, had utterly become one of the child people, suffering because of a person, loving a person, lost in that love, a fool for love. Now, though late in his life, for once he too felt this strongest and strangest passion, suffered from it, suffered lamentably, and yet was blessed, was somewhat renewed, somewhat richer.[14]

Of course he felt that this love, this blind love for his son was a passion, something extremely human, that it was samsara, a muddy wellspring, a dark water. And yet, at the same time he felt it was not worthless, it was necessary, originating in his own being. Even this pleasure must be atoned for, even these pains must be experienced, even these follies committed.

The son meanwhile let him commit his follies, let him compete for his affections, let him humiliate himself daily before his moods. This father had no qualities that enchanted him and none that he feared. He was a good man, this father, a good, kind, gentle man, perhaps a very pious man, maybe a saint—none of these qualities could win the boy. This father bored him, this man who held him captive in his miserable hut, he bored the boy, and that he met every bad habit with a smile, every insult with friendliness, every malicious act with benevolence, this itself was the old conniver's most hateful trick. The boy would much rather have been threatened or abused by him.

There came a day on which the young Siddhartha openly declared himself and turned against his father. His father had given him the task of collecting brushwood. But the boy would not leave the hut, he stood there stubborn and fuming, stamped the ground, balled up his fists, and in a mighty outburst of hatred and contempt screamed in his father's face.

"Go and get your own brushwood!" he cried out, foaming at the mouth, "I am not your servant. I know you will not strike me, you would not dare to; I know that with your piety and consideration you constantly wish to punish me and make me small. You think I should be like you, just as pious, just as soft, just as wise! But I, listen to me, what I want is to make you suffer, I would rather be a bandit and a murderer and go to hell than to be like you! I hate you; you are not my father, even if you were my mother's lover ten times over!"

Rage and grief spilled out of him, seething in a hundred desolate and angry words toward his father. Then the boy ran, not returning until late in the evening.

But the next morning he was gone. Gone too was a small, two-colored basket woven of bast fiber, in which the ferrymen had kept those copper and silver coins they had received in payment for the ferry. Gone as well was the boat, Siddhartha saw it lying on the opposite bank of the river. The boy had run away.

"I must follow him," said Siddhartha, who still trembled miserably since the boy had used abusive language on the prior day. "A child cannot walk through the woods alone. He will perish. We must build a raft, Vasudeva, to get across the water."

"We will build a raft," Vasudeva replied, "in order to reclaim our boat, which the young man has carried off. But my friend, you should let him go, he is no longer a child, he knows how to fend for himself. He is looking for the road to the city, and he is right, do not forget this. He is doing what you have neglected to do. He is taking care of himself, he is on his own track. Oh, Siddhartha, I see you are suffering, but you suffer pains over things that should make one laugh, over things that will soon make you laugh."

Siddhartha did not answer. He already held the axe in his hands, and began to make a raft out of bamboo and Vasudeva helped him bind the stalks together with grass ropes. Then they traveled across, drifted far, pulled the raft upstream along the opposite river bank.

"Why have you brought the axe along?" asked Siddhartha.

Vasudeva answered: "It may be that our boat's oar has been lost."

But Siddhartha knew what his friend was thinking. He thought the boy would have thrown the oar away or broken it, to take his revenge and to impede their pursuit. And truly there was no oar in the boat. Vasudeva pointed to the bottom of the boat and smiled at his friend, as if to say: "Don't you see what your son wants to tell you?

Don't you see that he does not want to be pursued?" And yet he did not say this with words. He busied himself carving a new oar. Siddhartha, though, took his leave in order to search for the runaway. Vasudeva did not prevent him.

When Siddhartha had already gone far into the forest, it entered his mind that his search was useless. Either, so he thought, the boy was far ahead of him and had already arrived in the city or, if he still were en route, he would keep himself hidden from his pursuer. As he went on thinking, he also realized he himself was not worried about his son; deep inside he knew that neither had he perished, nor did danger threaten him in the woods. Nonetheless he went on without rest, no longer to save him, only out of the desire perhaps to see him again. And he walked to the edge of the city.

As he drew near the city on a broad road, he came to a halt at the entrance of the beautiful pleasure garden that once had belonged to Kamala, where he had seen her, in her palanquin, for the first time. Time gone by rose up in his soul: he saw himself standing there again, young, a naked shramana with a beard, his hair full of dust. For a long time Siddhartha stood and peered through the open gate into the garden, he saw monks in yellow cowls walking under the beautiful trees.

A long time he stood, contemplative, seeing images, hearkening to the story of his life. He stood there long, looked at the monks, instead of them he saw the young Siddhartha, saw the young Kamala walking under the tall trees. Clearly he saw himself, how Kamala took him in, how he received her first kiss, how proudly and contemptuously he looked back upon his Brahminhood, proudly and demandingly he began his worldly life. He saw Kamaswami, saw the servants, the feasting, the dice players, the musicians, saw Kamala's songbird in its cage, lived all this once again, breathed samsara, once again was old and tired, once again felt revulsion, once again felt the wish to extinguish himself, recovered once more with the holy Om.

After he had been standing at the garden gate for a long time, Siddhartha understood that the need that had driven him to this place was foolhardy, that he could not help his son, that he must not cling to him. Deep in his heart he felt the love he had for the runaway was like a wound, and at the same time he felt the wound was not given to him for probing, it was meant to blossom and be resplendent.

That the wound at this hour did not yet flourish, did not yet shine, made him sad. In place of his fondest desire, which had drawn him to this place and in pursuit of his runaway son, now there was emptiness. Sadly he sat down, feeling something in his heart die, sensing emptiness, seeing no more joy, no goal. He sat immersed in meditation, and waited. This he had learned by the river, this one thing: to wait, to have patience, to listen. And he sat listening, in the dust of the road, listening to his heart, how tiredly and sadly it beat, waiting for a voice. Many an hour he crouched there listening, no longer seeing visions, he sank into the emptiness, let himself sink, without seeing a path. And when he felt the wound burning, soundlessly he spoke the Om, filled himself with Om. The monks in the garden saw him, and as he stooped there for many hours, and dust gathered on his gray hair, one of them came and lay two plantains down before him. The old man did not see him.

Out of this torpor a hand awakened him, touching his shoulder. Immediately he recognized this gentle, bashful touch, and he came to. He rose up and greeted Vasudeva, who had come after him. And then he gazed into Vasudeva's friendly face, into the tiny wrinkles filled with nothing but smiles, into the bright eyes, then he too smiled. Now he saw the plantains lying before him, picked them up, gave one to the ferryman, ate the other himself. Then he got up silently with Vasudeva and went back into the forest, returned home to the ferry. Neither of them spoke of what had happened on this day, neither of them mentioned the boy's name, neither spoke of his flight, neither spoke of the wound. In the hut Siddhartha lay down on his bed and a little while later, when Vasudeva walked over to him to offer a bowl of coconut milk, he found him already asleep.

# OM

For a long time the wound still burned. Siddhartha had to transport many a traveler who had a son or a daughter along across the river, and there was not one he regarded without envy, without thinking: "So many, so many thousands are so graciously favored—why not I? Even wicked people, even thieves and robbers have children, and love them, and are loved by them, I alone am not." He thought so simply now, so mindlessly, he had become so similar to the child people.

He looked at people differently than he did before, less cleverly, less proudly, and thus with greater warmth, with greater curiosity, engaging more with them. When he transported the usual types of travelers—child people, business people, warriors, womenfolk—these people did not seem alien to him as they once did: he understood them, he understood and did not share their thoughts and insights, but like them he had the feel of a life driven solely by impulses and desires. Although he was nearing perfection, and endured his final wound, it still seemed to him these child people were his brothers; their vanity, covetousness, and ludicrousness had lost their absurdity for him, had become comprehensible, lovable, even worthy of esteem. A mother's blind love for her child, an educated father's idiotic blind pride in his only little son, an idle young woman's blind and frantic pursuit of jewels and the admiring eyes of men, all these impulses, all these childish matters, all these simple, foolhardy or monstrously strong, extremely vivid, strongly opposing drives and desires were no longer childish things for Siddhartha now; he saw people live for their sake, saw them accomplish infinitely difficult tasks for their sake, make journeys, wage wars, suffer endlessly, endure endlessly, and he could love them for that; he saw life, vivacity, the indestructible, Brahman in every one of their passions, every one of their deeds. In their blind faith, their blind strength and tenacity these people were lovable and admirable. They lacked nothing; the wise man and the thinker had nothing on them but one single triviality, one single extremely tiny thing: the consciousness, the conscious thought of the unity of all life. And there were many hours when even Siddhartha doubted whether this knowledge, this thought should be so highly valued, whether it too were not perhaps a trifle of the thought people, of the thought-child people. In all other ways worldly people were born equal to the wise, often they were superior to them, just as animals too can appear superior to people in the tenaciousness of their unflinching actions at moments of necessity.

Slowly it blossomed, and slowly too it ripened in Siddhartha, the knowledge, the knowing that was actually wisdom, concerning the goal of his long seeking. It was nothing but a readiness of the soul, a capability, a secret art, to think the thought of unity at every moment in life, to be able to feel and inhale unity. Slowly this unfolded within him, streamed back at him from Vasudeva's aged childlike face: harmony, knowledge of the eternal perfection of the world, the smile, unity.

But the wound still burned, passionately and bitterly Siddhartha thought of his son, nursing the love and affection in his heart, allowing the pain to feed on itself, committing all the follies of love. Not of itself did this flame go out.

And one day, with the wound burning intensely, Siddhartha crossed the river, driven by longing, and got out of the boat with his mind set on going to the city and searching for his son. The river ran softly and gently, it was the dry season, but its voice sounded strange: it was laughing! It was definitely laughing. The river laughed, bright and clear it laughed at the old ferryman. Siddhartha stopped still, he bent down over the water to hear better, and in the tranquil pull of the water he saw his face mirrored, and the reflection of his face reminded him of something, something he had forgotten, and brooding over it, he realized: this face resembled another he once knew and loved and also feared. It resembled the face of his father, the Brahmin. And he remembered, how back then, a youth, he had forced his father to let him to go to the penitents, how he had taken leave of him, how he left and never again returned. Had not his father also suffered the same pain over him as he now was suffering over his son? Had not his father died a long time ago, alone, without having seen his son again? Must he himself not await the same fate? Was it not a comedy, was there not something strange and stupid about this repetition, this running in a fatal circle?

The river laughed. Yes, it was so, it all came back, everything not suffered through to the end and resolved, the same woes were suffered again and again. Siddhartha, however, climbed back into the boat and steered back to the hut, remembering his father, remembering his son, ridiculed by the river, quarreling with himself, leaning toward despair, and no less inclined to laugh along out loud at himself and all the world. Alas, the wound was not yet blossoming, his heart still bridled against fate, cheerfulness and victory did not yet radiate from his affliction. On the contrary, he felt hope, and when he had returned to the hut, he felt an invincible longing to open himself before Vasudeva, to reveal everything to him, the master of listening, to tell him everything.

Vasudeva sat inside the hut weaving a basket. He no longer drove the ferry, his eyes had begun to grow weak, and not only his eyes but also his arms and hands. The only thing that was unaltered and blossoming was the joy and bright benevolence of his face.

Siddhartha sat down near the old man, slowly he began to speak. He spoke now of things they had never discussed, of his going to the city, back then, of the burning wound, of his envy at the sight of happy fathers, of his knowing the folly of such wishes, of his vain battle against them. He reported all this, he could simply say it all, even the most painful things, everything said itself, everything manifested itself, he could tell all. He displayed his wound, told also of today's flight, how today he had been taken across the water, a childish refugee, intending to walk through the city, how the river had laughed.

While he spoke, spoke on and on, while Vasudeva listened with a serene face, Siddhartha experienced Vasudeva's listening more strongly than he had ever felt it; he sensed how his pains, his anxieties flowed over, how his secret hope flowed over, and came back to him again from the other side. Showing his wound to this listener was the same as bathing it in the river, until it became cool and was united with the river. While he went on speaking, went on revealing himself and confessing, Siddhartha increasingly felt this was no longer Vasudeva, no longer a human being who listened to him; the motionless listener absorbed his confession as a tree does the rain, the motionless one was itself the river, was itself god, was itself the eternal. And while Siddhartha ceased thinking about himself and his wound, the knowledge of the altered essential being of Vasudeva took possession of him, and the more he sensed it and immersed himself in it, the less strange it became, the more he realized that everything was in its natural order, that Vasudeva had already been this way for a long time, almost always, that only he himself had not entirely recognized it, yes, that he himself could scarcely still be distinguished from the other. He sensed he was now seeing the old Vasudeva the way people see the gods, and that this could not last; in his heart he began to take leave of Vasudeva. All the while he went on talking.

When he had spoken his fill, Vasudeva aimed his friendly, somewhat weak gaze upon him, said nothing, silently beaming toward him love and cheerfulness, appreciation and knowledge. He took Siddhartha's hand, led him to their seat by the riverbank, sat down with him, smiled toward the river.

"You have heard it laugh," he said. "But you have not heard everything. Let us listen together, there is more that you will hear."

They listened. The many-voiced song of the river sounded softly. Siddhartha gazed into the water, and as the water moved images came to him: his father appeared, alone, sorrowing over his son; he himself appeared, alone, also bound with the bands of longing for his distant son; his son appeared, he too alone, the boy, desirous, raging on the burning track of his young wishes, each one of them aiming for his goal, each one possessed by his goal, each one suffering. The river sang with a voice of pain, it sang passionately, it flowed ardently toward its goal, its voice sounded like a lament.

"Do you hear it?" Vasudeva's mute gaze asked. Siddhartha nodded.

"Listen more closely!" Vasudeva whispered.

Siddhartha took pains to listen harder. The image of his father, his own image, the image of his son flowed into one another, Kamala's image also appeared and dissolved, and the image of Govinda, and other images, and they all flowed into and over one another, all of them became the river, all strove as a river toward its goal, fervent, coveting, suffering, and the river's voice sounded full of longing, full of scorching pain, full of craving that could not be stilled. The river strove toward its goal, Siddhartha saw it rush there, the river that was made of him and his kin and every human being he had ever seen, all the waves and waters made haste, suffering, toward destinations, many of them, to the waterfall, to the lake, to the rapids, to the sea, and all the goals were reached, and a new one followed each, and out of the water came vapor and rose into the heavens, came rain and plummeted down from the sky, came wellspring, came brook, came river, striving anew, flowing anew. But the ardent voice had changed. It still resounded, full of suffering, full of seeking, but other voices joined in, voices of joy and of pain, voices both good and ill, laughing and sorrowing, hundreds of voices, thousands of voices.

Siddhartha listened. Nothing but listener now, immersed in hearing, entirely empty, taking everything in, absorbing, he felt he had now learned everything there was to learn about listening. He had often heard all these many voices in the river; today it all sounded new. He could no longer distinguish the many voices, not the gay from the weeping, not the childish from the manly, they all belonged together, lamentation of longing and laughter of the wise, outcry of rage and moaning on the deathbed, everything was one, everything was interwoven and intricately knotted, a thousandfold. And everything together, all the voices, all the goals, all the yearning, all the suffering, all the desire, everything good and evil, everything all together was the world. Everything all together was the flow of events, was the music of life. And if Siddhartha listened attentively to this river, to this song of a thousand voices, if he did not listen to the pain or the laughter, if he did not bind his soul to any one voice and enter into it with his I, but rather listened to all, the entirety, perceiving the unity, then the great song of the thousand voices consisted of one single word, and the word was *OM*: perfection.[15]

"Do you hear it," Vasudeva's gaze asked again.

Brightly shone Vasudeva's smile, hovering above all the wrinkles of his aged countenance, luminous, just as the Om hovered over all the voices of the river. Brightly shone his smile, when he looked at his friend, and brightly now too the same smile gleamed on Siddhartha's face. His wound blossomed, his pain radiated, his I had flowed into the unity.

In this hour Siddhartha ceased struggling with his fate, ceased suffering. On his face blossomed the serenity of knowledge, which no will opposes any longer, knowing perfection, in agreement with the flow of events, with the stream of life, full of compassion, full of sympathy, abandoned to the flow, belonging to unity.

When Vasudeva rose from his seat on the riverbank, when he gazed into Siddhartha's eyes and saw the serenity of knowledge beaming in them, in his cautious and tender way, he gently touched Siddhartha's shoulder with his hand and said: "I have waited for this moment, dear friend. Now that it has come, let me go. For a long time I have waited for this moment, for a long time I have been Vasudeva the ferryman. Enough now, the time has come. Farewell, hut, farewell, river, farewell, Siddhartha!"

Siddhartha bowed down low before the departing man.

"I knew it," he said softly. "You will go into the woods?"

"I will go into the woods, I will go into unity," Vasudeva spoke, radiant.

Radiant he walked away; Siddhartha gazed after him. With deep joy, deeply earnest, he followed him with his gaze, saw his steps full of peace, saw his head full of splendor, saw his form full of light.

# GOVINDA

Once during a period of rest, Govinda lingered with other monks in the pleasure grove that the courtesan Kamala had presented to Gautama's disciples. He had heard about an old ferryman who lived a day's journey away, on the river, and whom many took for a wise man. When Govinda returned to the road, he chose the path to the ferry, eager to see this ferryman. For although he had lived his whole life according to the precepts, and was regarded by younger monks with the reverence due his age and his modesty, disquiet and seeking were still not extinguished in his heart.

He came to the river, he asked the old man to transport him, and when they disembarked on the opposite shore, he said to the old man: "You have done us monks and pilgrims a lot of good, you have already carried many of us across. Are you not also, Ferryman, a seeker after the right path?"

Siddhartha spoke, smiling out of his old eyes: "Do you call yourself a seeker, o Venerable One, you who are already advanced in years, and who wear the robe of the monks of Gautama?"

"Certainly I am old," said Govinda, "but I have not stopped seeking. Never will I stop seeking, this seems to be my calling. You, too, it seems to me, have been a seeker. Will you tell me something, Revered One?"

Siddhartha spoke: "Whatever would I have to tell you, Venerable One? Perhaps that you seek far too much? That because of your seeking you will not arrive at finding?"

"What is it you are saying?" asked Govinda.

"When someone seeks," Siddhartha answered, "then it happens all too easily that his eyes will see only the thing he is seeking, that he cannot find anything, cannot let anything in, because he is always thinking only of that thing he seeks, because he has a goal, because he is possessed by the goal. Seeking means: having a goal. But finding means: being free, being open, having no goal. You, Venerable One, may indeed be a seeker, for, striving toward your goal, there is much you do not see which is right before your eyes."

"I still do not entirely understand you," Govinda asked, "just what do you mean?"

Siddhartha continued: "Once, o Venerable One, many years ago, you were at this very river, and at this river you found a sleeper, and you sat by him to watch over his sleep. However, o Govinda, you did not recognize the sleeper."

Astonished, like someone under a spell, the monk looked into the eyes of the ferryman.

"Are you Siddhartha?" he asked in a shy voice. "I would not have recognized you this time either! From my heart I greet you, Siddhartha, wholeheartedly I am glad to see you again! You have changed a great deal, Friend.—And so now you have become a ferryman?"

Siddhartha laughed amiably. "A ferryman, yes. Many people, Govinda, must go through a lot of changes, must wear all sorts of robes, I am one of them, dear friend. Welcome, Govinda, please spend the night in my hut."

Govinda spent the night in the hut and slept in the bed that once was Vasudeva's. He addressed many questions to the friend of his youth, Siddhartha had to tell him many stories from his life.

The next morning, when it was time to take up his daily wandering, not without hesitation Govinda pronounced the words: "Before I continue on my way, Siddhartha, permit me one more question. Do you have a doctrine? Do you have a creed, or a Veda, which you follow, that helps you live and act correctly?"

Siddhartha spoke: "You know, dear friend, that already as a young man, back when we were both living in the forest with the penitents, I came to distrust teachings and teachers and I turned my back on them. My thoughts and feelings have remained the same. Nonetheless, since then I have had many teachers. A beautiful courtesan was my instructress for a long time, and a wealthy businessman was my teacher, and a few dice players. Once, too, a wandering disciple of Buddha was my teacher; he was on a pilgrimage and he sat beside me, when I had fallen asleep in the woods. From him too I learned, to him too I am thankful, very thankful. But I have learned most of all from this river, and from my predecessor, the ferryman Vasudeva. He was a very simple man, Vasudeva, he was no thinker, but he knew what was necessary just as well as Gautama, he had attained perfection, he was a saint."

Govinda said: "As ever, o Siddhartha, it seems you still have some love of scorn. I believe you and know that you have not followed a teacher. But have you not, even if you have not found a doctrine, have you not yourself had certain thoughts, certain insights that are your own and help you to live? If you would confide to me something of this, it would gladden my heart."

Siddhartha spoke: "I have had thoughts, yes, and insights, ever and always. Sometimes, for an hour or for a day, I have felt knowledge within me, just as one feels life within his heart. There were many thoughts, but it would be difficult for me to convey them. You see, my Govinda, here is one of the thoughts I have found: Wisdom cannot be conveyed. The wisdom a sage attempts to convey always sounds like folly."

"Are you joking?" Govinda asked.

"I am not joking. I am telling you what I have found. One can convey knowledge but not wisdom. One can find wisdom, one can live it, one can be borne by it, one can work wonders with it, but one can neither speak it nor teach it. This is what at times I surmised even in my youth, what drove me away from my teachers. I have discovered a thought, Govinda, which again you will take as a joke or as folly, but which is my finest: The opposite of every truth is equally true! To wit: a truth always only allows itself to be expressed and wrapped in words when it is unilateral. Everything that can be thought with thoughts and said with words is unilateral, everything one-sided, a moiety, everything lacks wholeness, roundness, unity. When the exalted Gautama, teaching, spoke of the world, he had to divide it into samsara and nirvana, into illusion and truth, into suffering and release. One can do nothing else, there is no other way for the one who wants to teach. But the world itself, that which exists around us and inside us, is never unilateral. Never is a man or a deed wholly samsara or wholly nirvana, never is a person entirely saintly or entirely sinful. It only seems so, because we are subject to the illusion that time is something real. Time is not real, Govinda, I have experienced this often, very often. And if time is not real, then the span that seems to lie between world and eternity, between suffering and bliss, between evil and good, also is an illusion."

"How so?" Govinda asked anxiously.

"Listen well, dear friend, listen well! The sinner that I am and that you are, he is a sinner but he will again be Brahma, one day he will attain nirvana, will be Buddha—and now look: this 'one day' is an illusion, it is only a metaphor! The sinner is not on the path to Buddhahood, he is not in a process of development, although our thoughts have no other way to imagine these things. No, in the sinner, now and today the future Buddha already exists, his future is already entirely there, you must revere the becoming, the potential, the hidden Buddha in him, in yourself, in everyone. The world, Govinda my friend, is not imperfect, not to be seen as on a slow path toward perfection: No, it is perfect in every moment, all transgression already bears grace within itself, all little children already have the aged in themselves, all sucklings death, all the dying eternal life. It is not possible for any person to see how far on his path anyone else may be; in the bandit and the dice player waits Buddha, in the Brahmin waits the bandit. In deep meditation it is possible to stop time, to see all past, present and future life as simultaneous, and everything is good then, everything perfect, everything is Brahman. For that reason to me it seems what *is* appears good, death as life, transgression as holiness, cleverness as foolishness; everything must be so, requiring only my acceptance, only my willingness, my loving accord, for it to be good for me, to work for my benefit, never able to harm me. With body and soul I have experienced my own great need to sin, to seek pleasure, to strive for possessions, to be indolent, and a need for the most shameful despair, in order to learn to cede my resistance, to learn to love the world, to learn no longer to compare it to a world I desired and imagined, to some preconceived sort of perfection, rather to leave it as it is, to love it, and to enjoy belonging to it.—These, o Govinda, are a few of the thoughts that have entered my mind."

Siddhartha bent over, picked a stone up off the ground and weighed it in his hand.

"This here," he said playfully, "is a stone, and at a specified time perhaps it will be earth, and from the earth will come a plant, or an animal, or a human. Now earlier I would have said: 'This stone is nothing but a stone, it is worthless, it belongs to the world of Maya; but because in the round of transformation it can perhaps also become human and spirit, thus I also grant it value.' Maybe that's how I would have thought before. But today I think: this stone is stone, it is also animal, it is also god, it is also Buddha, I do not revere and love it because it could one day become this or that, rather because long ago and always it *is* everything—and just this, that it is stone, that to me now and today it appears as stone, precisely for that reason I love it, and see value and meaning in every one of its veins and hollows, in the yellow, in the gray, in the hardness, in the sound it makes if I tap it, in the dryness or moistness of its surface. There are stones that feel like oil or soap, and others like leaves, others like sand, and every one is special and prays the Om in its way, every one is Brahman, but at the same time and equally much it is stone, oily or moist, and precisely this pleases me and seems wondrous and worthy of adoration. —But let me say no more. Words do the secret sense no good, it always goes somewhat off when one utters it aloud, it sounds somewhat false, somewhat foolish—yes, and this too is very good and pleases me greatly, I also greatly agree with the following statement: What is a treasure and wisdom to one man always sounds like utter foolishness to another."

In silence Govinda listened.

"Why have you told me about the stone?" he asked hesitantly after a pause.

"It happened unintentionally. Or perhaps it is just that I love even the stone and the river and all these things we observe and from which we can learn. I can love a stone, Govinda, and also a tree or a piece of its bark. These are things and one can love things. But I cannot love words. That is why teachings are not for me, they have no hardness, no softness, no colors, no edges, no smell, no taste, they have nothing but words. Maybe this is what prevents you from finding peace, maybe it is the many words. For even release and virtue, even samsara and nirvana are only words, Govinda. There is no thing that would be nirvana; there is only the word nirvana."

Govinda spoke: "Nirvana, Friend, is not only a word. It is a thought."

Siddhartha went on: "A thought, it may be so. I must confess to you, dear friend: I hardly distinguish between thoughts and words. Candidly speaking, I do not put much store in thoughts either. I put more into things. Here on this ferryboat, for example, was a man, my predecessor and teacher, a holy man, who for many long years simply believed in the river, nothing else. He had noticed that the voice of the river spoke to him, he learned from it, it reared and instructed him, to him the river seemed a god, for many long years he did not know that every wind, every cloud, every bird, every beetle is just as divine and knows and can teach just as much as the revered river. When this saint, however, went into the woods, then he knew it all, knew more than you and I, with no teachers, no books, only because he had believed in the river."

Govinda said: "But what you call 'things,' are they something real, something essential? Is this not the illusion of Maya, only image and semblance? Your stone, your tree, your river—are these objects real things then?"

"This does not trouble me very much either," Siddhartha replied. "Maybe things all are semblance, maybe not; very well, then I too am only semblance, and so too are all those of my kind. That is what makes them so dear and estimable to me: they are like me. That is why I can love them. And this is now a lesson, about which you will laugh: Love, o Govinda, seems to me the matter principal, foremost of all. To see through the world, to explain it, to hold it in contempt, these may be matters for great thinkers. But the one thing that concerns me is the ability to love the world, not to hold it in contempt, not to hate it and myself, to be able to regard it and myself and all beings with love and admiration and reverence."

"This I comprehend," said Govinda. "But even this the Exalted One has identified as deception. He demands benevolence, protection, compassion, tolerance, but not love; he forbade us to shackle our hearts with love for the earthly."

"I know," said Siddhartha, his smile radiating golden. "I know that, Govinda. And see, we are in the midst of the thicket of opinion, in the battle over words. For I cannot lie, my words about love stand in opposition, in apparent opposition to Gautama's words. That is precisely why I distrust words so much, for I know this contradiction is an illusion. I know that I am at one with Gautama. How then should He too not know love, He who has recognized all humanity in its transience, in its nothingness, and has yet so greatly loved humankind that he has devoted a long life full of toil exclusively to helping them, to teaching them! Even in him, even in your great teacher, I prefer the thing to the words, his actions and his life are more important than his speech, the gestures of his hand more important than his opinions. Not in speech, not in thought do I see his greatness, only in his actions, in his life."[16]

For a long time the two old men kept silent. Then Govinda spoke, while he bowed to take his leave: "I thank you, Siddhartha, for telling me some of your thoughts. They are partly strange thoughts, not all of them were immediately comprehensible to me. Be that as it may, I thank you, and I wish you peaceful days."

(But to himself secretly he thought: This Siddhartha is a strange person, strange thoughts he pronounces, his teaching sounds foolish. The pure teachings of the Exalted One sound different, clearer, purer, more understandable, with nothing peculiar, foolhardy or ridiculous in them. But Siddhartha's hands and feet, his eyes, his brow, his breathing, his smile, his greeting, his gait seem different to me from his thoughts. Never since our exalted Gautama entered into nirvana, never have I encountered such a man of whom I have felt: this is a saint! Only him, I have found only this Siddhartha. Maybe his teaching is strange, maybe his words sound foolish, his gaze and his hand, his skin and his hair, everything about him radiates a purity, a calm, radiates a serenity and mildness and holiness, which I have not seen in any other human being since the final death of our exalted teacher.)

While Govinda thought thus, and a conflict occurred in his heart, he bowed again to Siddhartha, drawn by love. Deeply he bowed down to the one who sat there calmly composed.

"Siddhartha," he said, "we are old men now. I can hardly believe we will see each other again in this form. I see, beloved friend, that you have found peace. I admit that I have not found it. Tell me, Revered One, one more thing, give me something I can take with me, that I can hold on to and understand. Give me something to take with me on my way. My path is often difficult, often dark, Siddhartha."

Siddhartha remained silent and looked at him always with the same, tranquil smile. Rigidly Govinda stared into his face, with fear, with longing; pain and eternal seeking were inscribed in his gaze, eternal not-finding.

Siddhartha saw this and smiled.

"Bend over to me!" he whispered softly into Govinda's ear. "Bend down to me here! Here, even closer! Come closer still! Kiss me on the forehead, Govinda!"

But while Govinda in bewilderment, and nonetheless drawn by great love and anticipation, obeyed his words, bowing near to him and touching his forehead with his lips, something wonderful happened to him. While his thoughts lingered on Siddhartha's strange words, while he was still vainly struggling with his own reluctance to think time away, imagining nirvana and samsara as one, while even a certain contempt for his friend's words battled within him against a terrible love and awe, this is what happened to him:

He no longer saw the face of his friend Siddhartha, instead he saw other faces, many, a long series, a streaming river of faces, of hundreds, thousands, all of which came and went past, and yet all of which simultaneously appeared to be there, all of which continually transformed and renewed themselves, and yet all of which were Siddhartha. He saw the face of a fish, of a carp, with a mouth opened in infinite pain, of a dying fish, its eyes clouding over—he saw the face of a newborn child, red and full of creases, contorted with weeping—he saw the face of a murderer, saw him stick a knife into the body of another man—he saw, at the same moment, the same criminal kneel in chains and saw his head hewn off by a single stroke of the executioner's sword—he saw the naked bodies of men and women in postures and battles of raging love—he saw corpses laid out, still, cold, empty—he saw heads of animals, of boars, crocodiles, elephants, of bulls, of birds—he saw gods, Krishna, Agni—he saw all these figures and faces together in thousands of relationships to one another, each one helping the other, loving, hating, destroying, giving birth anew, each one was a death-wish, a passionate painful acknowledgment of transience, and yet not one died, each one simply metamorphosed, was continually born anew, always got a new face, without any time elapsing between faces—and all these figures and faces rested, flowed, engendered themselves, swam away and streamed into one another, and over them all there was constantly something thin, insubstantial, and yet something present, drawn out thin like a piece of glass or ice, like a transparent hide, a shell or form or mask of water, and this mask smiled, and this mask was Siddhartha's smiling face, which he, Govinda, at this very same moment touched with his lips. And, so Govinda saw, this smile of the mask, this smile of unity above the streaming forms, this smile of simultaneity above the thousand births and deaths, this smile of Siddhartha's was exactly like, was exactly the same, tranquil, fine, impenetrable, perhaps benevolent, perhaps scornful, wise, thousandfold smile of Gautama, of the Buddha, as he himself had beheld it with awe hundreds of times. This, Govinda knew, was how the Perfect Ones smiled.[17]

No longer knowing if time existed, if this vision had lasted a second or a hundred years, no longer knowing if Siddhartha existed, if Gautama existed, if an I and You existed, as if wounded deep inside by a divine arrow whose injury tastes sweet, casts a spell and dissolves deep inside, Govinda stood a little while yet, bending over Siddhartha's tranquil face, which he had just kissed, which just now had served as a stage on which all forms made their appearance, a stage for all becoming, for all being. The countenance was unchanged, after the great depth of the thousandfold forms had closed itself off again under its surface; he smiled quietly, smiled gently and softly, perhaps very benevolently, perhaps very scornfully, just as he had smiled, the Exalted One.

Govinda bowed low; tears, of which he knew nothing, ran down over his old face; the feeling of most intimate love, of most humble reverence burned like a fire in his heart. Deeply he bowed, down to the earth, before the one who sat motionless, whose smile reminded him of everything he had ever loved in all his life, everything he had ever in all his life valued and held sacred.

# NOTES

## Part One

1. (p. 5) *Siddhartha:* Siddhartha means "One who has accomplished his aim." It is the name of the Shakya prince, Siddhartha Gautama, who became the Shakyamuni Buddha at the age of thirty-five, probably in the sixth century B.C. Hesse's choice of this name for his hero is highly significant; along with many of his contemporaries, Hesse was drawn to the Buddha and wanted to tell the story of his quest for enlightenment. At the same time, however, Hesse believed that an individual must find enlightenment for himself: an overarching theme of his thought is the importance of the individual over the group. Thus Hesse's hero is another Siddhartha, a contemporary of the Buddha, who follows the Buddha's example by not following him personally.

2. (p. 5) *the handsome son of the Brahmin:* As a Brahmin, Siddhartha is a Hindu of the highest caste, a member of the priestly or intellectual class of ancient India. Brahmins are servants of Brahma, the Creator in Vedic Indian theism, and seekers of *Brahman*, the impersonal ultimate reality of all things for the later religious form of Vedantism. This points to another difference between Siddhartha Gautama, who became the Buddha, and Hesse's Siddhartha, since Siddartha Gautama was born into the warrior class, of royal lineage and duty.

3. (p. 5) *Govinda, his friend:* Govinda (Sanskrit for "cowherd") is a name of Krishna, the eighth incarnation of the Hindu god Vishnu, who is the focus of a dominant strand of Indian monotheism of the last millennium and a half. Hesse probably also chose this name for Siddhartha's best friend because it is a common Indian name.

4. (p. 5) *Om:* OM is the prime mantra, or magic spell word, of Indic contemplatives; it consists of the sounds *a*, *u*, and *m*, which represent, respectively, body, speech, and mind of divine or enlightened reality. It invokes the absolute into the relative moment, and thus contains all sounds and begins all other prayers and invocations.

5. (p. 6) *among the radiant:* The "radiant" (in Sanskrit, *prabhasvara*) is the name of one of the highest strata of Indian heavens, of which there are

about twenty-six distinct levels in most cosmologies. Hesse's sources here are doubtless telling him that it is the heaven of Brahma the Creator; hence arriving among the radiant would, for Hesse, be equivalent to achieving the supreme insight into the nature of reality.

6. (p. 6) *verses of the Rig Veda:* The Rig Veda is the oldest collection of hymns in the Indian canon and the most important text of ancient Vedism (the word "Hinduism" is better applied to the later forms of Indian spirituality, influenced by Buddhism as well as by Vedism). Siddhartha would know many of these hymns by heart; some of them are beautiful poetry, solemnly chanted during the Brahmins' rituals.

7. (p. 7) *And what was the nature of the gods?:* Vedist cosmology includes the existence of many gods of natural forces, similar to the ancient Greek pantheon of Zeus and company. It also has the notion of a Creator, here called Prajapati, sometimes also called Brahma (see note 2, above). By the time of the Siddharthas, a revolutionary movement among Brahmins, associated with esoteric texts called Upanishads and with the discourses of non-Vedist Indian philosophers such as Jains and Buddhists, was considering all the outer gods to be but manifestations of the unitary reality of the I or Self (*Atman*). This led its followers to abandon external rituals and priestly status in order to seek within for one's own inner divinity and for absolute oneness with all divinity, the "Godhead."

8. (p. 7) *the Upanishads of the Sama Veda:* The Sama Veda is another collection of hymns, some almost the same as those in the Rig Veda, collected for the use of the chanting specialists in the Vedist rituals. This collection had its own set of esoteric Upanishad texts.

9. (p. 8) *Where was the initiate who could magically conjure intimacy with Atman from deep sleep into waking life, into every move, into every word and deed?:* The higher state of consciousness taught in the Upanishads was connected to ordinary consciousness in the following way: waking consciousness (syllable *a*), dreaming consciousness (syllable *u*), deep sleep consciousness (syllable *mmm*), and the supreme fourth consciousness (little dot of silence above the *mmm*, or the whole *OM*), each aware of all without duality. When you know your I as God, you know your soul as the whole world, and so on. The highest state of consciousness is reached when you know your I as God and your soul as the whole world. This experience was the object of Siddhartha's quest.

10. (p. 8) *a section of the Chandogya Upanishad:* The Chandogya Upanishad is one of the most important of these originally esoteric Vedist texts.

11. (p. 8) *"Yea, of this Brahman the name is Satyam—the True; he who knows*

*this enters every day into heaven"*: *Satya* is the Sanskrit term for truth, reality, being, what *is*. This realization could lead to heavenly experiences but is not just an entrance into "heaven," and heaven is not considered a final destination; *Satya* is rather an experience of the totality of everything, which renders any limited state, even a heavenly one, to a lesser reality. It is not certain that Hesse is totally clear about this key point, given both his Christian upbringing (wherein heaven is the final goal) and the variety of opinions on this in Indic religious thought. (The nature of the final achievement is a point of debate among Jains, Buddhists, Vedists, and various Indic monotheists, such as Shaivists, Vaishnavists, and others.)

12. (p. 9) *Thinking Om, his soul dispatched as an arrow toward Brahman:* Siddhartha here shows his special aptitude for the ultimate, in his spontaneous entrance into a complete contemplative trance even as a youth, without special training and long practice. The scene parallels a famous episode in the Buddha's youth: At a spring planting festival, the Buddha sat by himself under a tree and went into an advanced trance; this so frightened his father (who was already worried by a prediction that his son wouldn't become a warrior king and would instead go off to seek enlightenment) that for the next twenty years he made sure his son was never left alone.

13. (p. 9) *shramanas:* Hesse's original spelling of this word—*samanas*—is, scholars today would agree, incorrect. The word comes down to us in two different traditional languages, Sanskrit and Pali, each with its own transliterated spelling: from Sanskrit with an *r* after and a diacritical accent mark over the initial *s* and a diacritical dot under the n—*śramaṇa*—and from Pali with a diacritical dot under the *n*—*samaṇa*. For the present edition, we have chosen to substitute the accepted, easier to read (sans diacriticals), modern phonetic transliteration of the Sanskrit term for Hesse's original spelling of this and several other historical terms. For example we have used *Shakyamuni* for Hesse's *Sakyamuni*, *Shakya* for his *Sakya*, and *Gautama* for his *Gotama*. Our hope is that by standardizing the spellings in this way we both honor Hesse's original intent and make the historical aspects of his novel more accessible to the modern reader. [Publisher's Note]

14. (p. 9) *"He will become a shramana"*: Here we have Siddhartha's encounter with the wild ascetics called *shramanas*, professional seekers who have abandoned all normal living for the inner quest. This also parallels an incident in the Buddha's story, in which the soon-to-be-Buddha sees, one by one, an old person, a sick person, a corpse, and an ascetic, and then resolves to escape his princely life for the quest.

15. (p. 10) *"Tell me then what you have come here to say"*: This deeply moving scene between Siddhartha and his father is similar and also interestingly different from its model in the Buddha's life. Siddhartha Gautama also asked permission of his father to leave home for the ascetic's life, but his father flatly refused and even locked him up in the palace. Ultimately, Siddhartha had to disobey his father; in leaving, he abandoned his wife and child in a wrenching, revolutionary assertion of an individual's destiny over any group's call to duty. Hesse's Siddhartha has an easier time leaving, for his father never directly forbids him; still, he does break his father's heart, which he comes to realize long afterward. Considering Hesse's difficult youth, and the awful times he had been through with his first wife and children before he wrote this book, this scene poignantly evokes the struggle of the spiritual seeker to break away from binding family relationships.

16. (p. 13) *Life was affliction:* Siddhartha here explores the Buddha's First Noble Truth, that of suffering, which states that all unenlightened, egocentric existence is pain, in essence, part of the hopeless struggle between the individual and the opposing, separate universe.

17. (p. 16) *"he finds the same thing that Siddhartha and Govinda find when in their long exercises they seep out of their bodies, escaping, lingering in the not-I"*: Siddhartha begins to tire of the *shramana*'s path, realizing that he has not reached his goal. In spite of all his shamanic out-of-body experiences, trances, and self-denials, he has never escaped preoccupation with the personal self. Hesse confuses things by injecting the idea of "not-self" (*anatma*), which was the Buddha's term for the ultimate realization, the object of the transcendent wisdom of enlightenment. In other words, what the Upanishads called Supreme I or Self the Buddha called not-I or non-Self or, better, selflessness. Both terms refer to an experience of freedom from dichotomous self-differentiation, the Buddhists stressing its critical self-liberation aspect, the Vedists stressing its unitive aspect.

18. (p. 17) *nirvana:* Here is another instance of Hesse using Vedist and Buddhist terminology interchangeably. Nirvana was the Buddha's term for the "blowing out" of the flame of suffering, the release from the stress of fighting with the universe, the peace ensuing from the realization of selflessness. This was the Buddha's minimalist term for the supreme bliss he discovered in enlightenment, carefully distinguished from experiences of oneness with the world and also from experiences of nothingness or mere unconsciousness. The whole of the Buddhist path and the vast literature of Buddhist thought are engaged with the pursuit of the meaning and realization of nirvana.

19. (p. 17) *"There is, o my friend, only one knowledge, this is everywhere, this is Atman, in me and in you and in every single creature":* Siddhartha again uses *Atman*, the Indian word for "self," which is the goal of his quest (see note 7 above).

20. (p. 18) *Someone had appeared, someone named Gautama, the Exalted One, the Buddha:* At this the first mention of the Buddha, Hesse uses his clan name, Gautama, rather than his personal name as the Buddha, Shakyamuni; he makes no mention of the fact that Buddha's pre-enlightenment, princely name was Siddhartha.

21. (p. 18) *who within himself had overcome the suffering of the world and brought the wheel of rebirth to a standstill:* As described here, the goal of the spiritual quest is the inner conquest of sorrows and the "standstill" of "the cycle of rebirth"; this is how nirvana is referred to in Theravada Buddhism, the form of Buddhism first developed in India and maintained in Sri Lanka, Thailand, Burma, and Tibet. It is based on the presentation of the Four Noble Truths in the First Teaching, which treats *samsara* and nirvana as a real duality, focuses on monastic renunciation from the worldly life, and leads its practitioners to seek real escape from the world in a transcendental state of extinction. The question of how the stoppage of the painful cycle of rebirth (*samsara*) relates to the experience of universal oneness stays with Siddhartha, and with the reader, to the end.

22. (p. 19) *Much that was splendid and incredible would be told of him. . . . But his enemies and those who were nonbelievers said, this Gautama . . . is without erudition, knowing neither practice nor castigation:* In this passage, Hesse imagines most vividly how word of the Buddha must have spread around the country in his time. He notes, rightly, that the Buddha rejected both Brahmanic (priestly) ritualism and shramanic (ascetic) self-mortification, thus stirring the ire of both priests and ascetics in general, though most of his followers were drawn from one or the other kind of spiritual person.

23. (p. 19) *Even to the shramanas in the forest, even to Siddhartha, even to Govinda the legend had come, slowly, drop by drop, every drop heavy with hope, every drop heavy with doubt. . . . the eldest shramana was no friend of this story. . . . he had no respect for this Gautama:* Govinda and Siddhartha's abandonment of self-mortification, when they leave their *shramana* teacher, parallels the other Siddhartha's—the Buddha's—eventual abandonment of his six years of mortification: Govinda and Siddhartha break free upon hearing about the Buddha's attainment; the Buddha stopped because he came to feel it was another form of self-preoccupation, a kind of

inverse but still egocentric hedonism. Exactly what brought him to that realization is controversial. The Buddha's five ascetical companions were just as angry with him when he stopped as Siddhartha and Govinda's companions were.

24. (p. 21) *With that he drew close to the shramana. . . . The old man grew mute, his eyes were transfixed, his will was paralyzed, his arms hung limp, Siddhartha's enchantment left him utterly powerless. . . . And with thanks the youths reciprocated the bows, returned the wish, departing the place amidst these formalities:* This scene is both humorous and somewhat repugnant, as Siddhartha shows off his ascetic powers by dominating the will of his old ascetic teacher. It is quite in keeping with Buddhist tradition, where such displays of psychic powers are considered distractions and side temptations, compared to the great aim of enlightenment.

25. (p. 24) *Siddhartha saw him, and recognized him immediately, as if a god had pointed the man out to him:* The phrase "as if a god had pointed the man out to him" is intriguing, as it shows how steeped Hesse was in Indic literature. It is a typical Indic, rather than a European, turn of phrase, born of a cosmology in which angel-like "godlets" (*devaputra*) are constantly present among the humans.

26. (pp. 24–25) *The Buddha went his way . . . an inviolable peace:* Hesse's first description of the Buddha bespeaks an instinct for reverence, though it also evinces his own view of what enlightenment must be. "Neither happy nor sad" does not accord with contemporary descriptions, which call the Buddha *Sugata*, or Blissful. The Buddha's gentle inward smile is fitting, though its childlike quality is imported from mysticism; in Buddhist literature, the Buddha is called Eldest of the World (*lokajyeshtha*).

27. (p. 25) *Siddhartha . . . was less curious about the teachings. . . . But he gazed attentively at Gautama's head. . . . This man, this Buddha, was true even down to the gesture of his little finger:* It is marvelous how Siddhartha receives teachings from the Buddha's body rather than his words. Hesse comes up with something deep here, though his European notion about Eastern mysticism and a Buddhist distaste for words miss the mark: As it turns out, Siddhartha "loves" the Buddha, his third father figure.

28. (pp. 25–26) *Gautama taught the lesson of suffering. . . . Whoever followed the path of the Buddha found release:* Hesse gets the Four Noble Truths right: (1) Unenlightened life is inevitable suffering, since self-centered pleasure is unstable; (2) the origin of that suffering is misperception of self as absolute, imprisoning the misperceiver in endless desire and hate; (3) there is a complete release from suffering, a reliable happiness, which is called nir-

vana; and (4) there is an eightfold way to nirvana. The eightfold path consists of two branches of wisdom (realistic worldview and intention), four branches of ethics (speech, evolutionary action, livelihood, and effort), and two branches of contemplative mind (mindfulness and concentration).

29. (p. 27) *"The teachings of the Exalted One are most excellent, how shall I find a single error in them?"*: Note here that Siddhartha's decision not to join the Buddha's community is not because of the Buddha's teachings, which he accepts as flawless, as far as any teachings can go.

30. (p. 27) *the youth summoned the courage to ask the Venerable One for permission to address him. Silently the Sublime One nodded to grant his request*: This encounter between Hesse's Siddhartha and the original Siddhartha, who had here become the Buddha, is crucial to understanding Hesse's intentions in the book. That Siddhartha has to pluck up courage to speak to the Buddha doesn't seem like normal behavior for him; Hesse himself seems to feel in this scene as if heís on a razor's edge.

31. (p. 28) *"you show the world as a single eternal chain, joined by cause and effect, as one perfect chain that is never and nowhere broken"*: I admire how Hesse has grasped the essential point that the Buddha's teaching is based on the discovery of cause and effect that frees the world from dependence on gods and from nihilistic randomness—a point often missed by those who think of Buddhism as a mysticism.

32. (p. 28) *"But now, according to your same teachings, this unity and logical consistency of all things nonetheless is interrupted at one place. . . . Please forgive me for uttering this objection"*: Though he had earlier told Govinda the Buddha's teachings were flawless, Siddhartha here perceives a contradiction in them: between the ultimate unity of the world and the rupture of that unity that makes possible the freedom from suffering that is nirvana. This is the difference between Vedist monism and Buddhist nondualism; Siddhartha (and Hesse) seem to be assuming that the Buddha agrees with the Vedist emphasis on monistic oneness, and thus cannot "prove" the possibility of selfless liberation. It looks bad for the Buddha!

33. (p. 29) *"You have heard the teachings, o Brahmin's son, and good for you that you have reflected so deeply. . . . This is what Gautama teaches, nothing else"*: The Buddha doesn't answer Siddhartha's objection directly; he withdraws from the ground of their metaphysical debate and disclaims any interest in persuading Siddhartha about anything, emphasizing the experiential dimension opened up by the teaching of nirvanic freedom.

34. (p. 29) *"no one attains deliverance through teaching!"*: In this passage Sid-

dhartha unilaterally withdraws his objection about duality versus unity, admitting it to be an "opinion," and accepts the coherence of the Buddha's teachings. But then he makes his main point: No teachings are ultimately useful; the Buddha didn't realize enlightenment from teachings, and no one can learn from teachings, as the "secret" is not there. The upshot is that in order to follow the Buddha, Siddhartha must not follow the Buddha! This individualistic ethos of the true seeker captures correctly a key aspect of the Buddhist quest, as opposed to the Vedist one. The Buddha's example is revolutionary in that it breaks away from Brahminic allegiance to the group. In fact, before the Buddha's time, the word *dharma* meant duty, law, and religion (patterns that maintain order), whereas after the Buddha, it came to mean reality, freedom, teaching, and practice (patterns that transcend order). There is, perhaps, a certain Zen influence here; Hesse might have heard something of the radical individualism of Zen Buddhism. However, Siddhartha seems to miss the point that teachings are there for individuals to use in their own self-reliant quest. Perhaps a Western (also Brahminic) idea of teaching as authoritarian transmission of formulaic knowledge causes Siddhartha and Hesse to miss the Buddhist sense of teachings—where teachings provide a liberating education in order to bring out the critical inner wisdom, ethical goodness, and experiential transformation in the individual.

35. (p. 30) *"return to the life of the world and of the passions?"*: The Buddha ends by warning Siddhartha about the dangers of becoming reengaged in the passions of the world. Remember that the Buddha had grown up a prince, indulged in every pleasure and passion; he had turned to asceticism, and then had rejected asceticism and adopted his mendicant's middle way, living simply but comfortably, midway between the world and the wilderness. Siddhartha, on the other hand, a solemn Brahmin's son who turned to harsh self-mortification, has not yet tasted the extremes of self-indulgence. This is a brilliant mirror-reversal.

36. (pp. 34–35) *The world was beautiful. . . . no longer the pointless and random multiplicity of the world of appearance, contemptible to the deep-thinking Brahmin, who scorns multiplicity, who seeks unity*: Siddhartha appreciates the diversity of the world; his own Brahmin tendency is to seek monistic unity. Hesse calls this return to diversity and the beauty of the world "awakening," and it completes Siddhartha's rebellions against the monism of his father, the asceticism of his *shramana* teacher, and the transcendentalism of the Buddha's Noble Truths. Giving up his third father, Siddhartha turns to Mother Nature.

37. (p. 35) *Blue was blue, river was river . . . and here Siddhartha:* In the midst of his newfound aestheticism, Siddhartha experiences a profound lack of identity, the paradoxical place the radical individualist discovers, where by becoming absolutely "himself" he becomes disconnected from everything. "As the sole star in the sky" (page 36), he dissolves into selflessness at a certain level.

## Part Two

1. (p. 41) *So to obey, not an external command, only the voice . . . nothing else was necessary:* What is the "inner voice" Siddhartha thinks Gautama was listening to under the bodhi tree? Is it like the "god" who pointed the Buddha out to Siddhartha in the Jetavana grove? Is it the I? Is it a voice of selfless wisdom?

2. (p. 41) *As the day began, Siddhartha asked his host the ferryman to take him across the river:* Take note of this wonderful ferryman, so casually introduced by Hesse. The dream Siddhartha has in the ferryman's hut reminds me of some of the poems Hesse wrote when he was in love with his eventual second wife, Ruth Wenger, after moving to Montagnola in southern Switzerland, where he wrote *Siddhartha*.

3. (p. 44) *he learned this was the grove of Kamala, the famous courtesan, and that beyond the grove she had a house in the city:* Siddhartha has fallen in love with first sight with Kamala ("lotus flower"), a beautiful courtesan. In India at that time, such a courtesan was more like a respected actress or movie star than a prostitute. Texts like the *Kamasutra* were already ancient by Siddhartha's time, and desire and pleasure were not considered evil or frightening, though they were temptations to be avoided by ascetics seeking transcendence. Kamala, the lotus flower, is thus the perfect teacher for the unteachable Siddhartha; she will show him the arts of love and humor.

4. (p. 48) *"You can read? And write?":* It is interesting that when Siddhartha lists his abilities, he mentions thinking, fasting, and waiting, and that it takes Kamala's intervention to extract reading and writing, the most important abilities for his worldly purpose.

5. (p. 49) *"You are expected at Kamaswami's, he is the wealthiest merchant in this city":* Kamaswami means "master of desire" in Sanskrit, and indeed this is Siddhartha's fifth teacher, teaching him the ways of business and wealth.

6. (p. 59) *"inside you is a stillness and a refuge, into which you can enter at any time and be at home, just as I can":* Hesse here betrays his feeling about enlightenment as something cold, individualistic, withdrawn, aloof—a result

of the limited sources on Buddhism available in his time. There was almost
no knowledge in the West about the Mahayana form of Buddhism, which
prevailed throughout the Buddhist world up to the end of the first millennium and still prevails in Tibet, China, and the Far East; this form stresses
compassion as well as wisdom, liberating engagement with the world as
well as transcendent liberation from the drives of the world.

7. (p. 61) *That high, bright alertness he had once experienced . . . had gradually become memory, had been transitory:* Here Siddhartha discovers that
the "high, bright alertness" he felt after leaving shramanahood, Govinda,
and the Buddha was not a true awakening. For if it were a true awakening, he would not have forgotten it, as he has now, in his life of pleasures,
his *samsara.*

8. (p. 68) *He smiled wearily, shook himself off and bade farewell to these things:*
This further renunciation is inspired by the famous scene in which the Siddhartha who became the Buddha, remaining awake after all the dancers
and musicians and revelers at his palace have passed out, looks at them
sleeping and feels revulsion toward the worldly pursuit of pleasure. By let-
ting Kamala become pregnant in her last round of passion with Siddhartha, Hesse provides a near-parallel with the Buddha leaving his
beloved wife, Yashodhara, just after the birth of their son, Rahula. I'm not
sure that Hesse consciously drew this parallel, yet it has a certain reso-
nance, demonstrating the total abandonment of all worldly ties that the
true seeker tends to practice.

9. (p. 70) *the very moment the Om penetrated his consciousness . . . he recognized himself in his misery and in his error:* Recalled from suicide by remembering the sound of *OM*, Siddhartha remembers that destroying the
body does not destroy life, which is indestructible. This makes even a dis-
solute and corrupted human life immensely valuable at least as a vehicle
for attaining freedom and enlightenment: If a life never dies, enlightenment is the only way out of suffering.

10. (p. 78) *But today he was young, the new Siddhartha was a child, and he was
full of joy:* Finally realizing that all Siddharthas are transitory, Siddhartha
comes closer to Buddhist selflessness; he thus adopts yet another "new Siddhartha" more lightly.

11. (p. 83) *Vasudeva:* Vasudeva (also Vasu) is a name of Vishnu, the supreme
God of all, in a dominant form of Indic monotheism. The name is also applied to Krishna, Vishnu's most beloved incarnation. Is it a reemergence of
Hesse's childhood, familial, culturally overarching monotheism that Siddhartha's final teacher (his fourth or fifth father, depending on whether we

count Kamaswami), from whom, finally, he does not run away, should be called "God"—God Vasudeva, the ultimate listener, the ferryman who takes us across the flood, who even refers us to the river itself?

12. (p. 85) *"Nothing was, nothing will be; everything is, everything has essence, is present"*: Siddhartha's insight about time—its unreality, its riverlike quality, its every moment containing all past and future and vice versa—is especially important and powerful. It is Hesse's great achievement.

13. (p. 91) *they built the funeral pyre:* The Buddha passes into Parinirvana. Or, as Mahayanists would say: He who has become eternally present everywhere out of transcendent wisdom and universal love for every being puts on the show of passing away from his distinct embodiment in order to teach people the lesson of the impermanence of everything. Kamala tries to go to the Buddha, is bitten by a snake on the way, and dies in Siddhartha's arms; she ends her life in Siddhartha's, rather than the Buddha's, presence, and returns her son to his father. This scene is deeply moving and deeply sad; yet I must say, with all this gathering of fathers and sons, I don't like the serpent *deus ex machina* doing away with the real live old woman, the beloved, mother, and teacher. River or no river, I think the woman's role and teachings are too vital to enlightenment, as well as to life.

14. (p. 97) *somewhat renewed, somewhat richer:* My respect for Hesse grows by leaps and bounds with this scene and Siddhartha's wonderful realization. Siddhartha's love for his son, helpless and foolish, connects with his memory of his proud and hurtful statement to Kamala that he could not love anyone. He realizes he does really love his son, and that he really has no "sanctuary," no place of aloofness within which to retreat from this love and dependence. German philosopher Friedrich Nietzsche, who through his writings was an intellectual mentor to Hesse, loved the Buddha too, and originally had him in mind as a model for his hero in his masterpiece *Thus Spake Zarathustra* (1883–1885). He switched to Zarathustra (better known as Zoroaster, the ancient Persian prophet) because he finally recoiled from the aloofness of the Buddha—an aloofness he learned from the Theravada, or monastic, form of Buddhism then known in Europe. He wanted an enlightenment that was joyous and life-affirming, and he was caught in the misleading negative stereotype of the Buddha. Nietzsche wanted a Mahayana vision for the Buddha, which he didn't know existed. Hesse is in the same territory here, and, though he understands Buddhism better than Nietzsche did, it may be another reason why his Siddhartha is pushed several steps beyond where Hesse thinks the Buddha arrived—steps specifically involving the human heart's endless capacity to love intensely and endlessly.

15. (p. 106) *if he did not bind his soul to any one voice and enter into it with his I, but rather listened to all, the entirety, perceiving the unity, then the great song of the thousand voices consisted of one single word, and the word was OM: perfection:* Here we have Siddhartha's final enlightenment, once again the great "going with the flow," the *OM* sound humming through the divine unity of all living. Siddhartha ceases "struggling with his fate" and is "in agreement with the flow of events, with the stream of life, full of compassion, full of sympathy, abandoned to the flow, belonging to unity." Here Hesse brings Siddhartha solidly along the Vedist path into the realization of Brahman (see note 2 to Part One), using images of surrender, merging, and flowing together. It is like what the great Buddhist lama Govinda (1898–1985) said: "Hinduism aims at the goal of each little drop merging and losing itself in the great ocean." Siddhartha is still caught in the mistake he made in talking to the Buddha in the Jetavana grove: He thinks that unity precludes the rupture of liberation. Intellectually, he misses the complexity of the Mahayana, where nonduality does not mean only oneness, but rather integrates oneness with duality. Mahayana wisdom is the constant awareness of freedom in unity, but it does not exclude love and compassion, which persist in duality. Not accepting the sufferings of the beloved, not settling for any sort of "as-it-is" about the world, but striving ceaselessly and skillfully to transform universes for the sake of lessening the suffering of beings and leading them to their own nondual awareness of freedom and sensitivity to the suffering of others—this is Mahayana wisdom. But I feel that Hesse emotionally catches this subtlety and complexity, which is why in his stories an exposure of the human heart always follows each unitive experience.

16. (p. 115) *"Not in speech, not in thought do I see his greatness, only in his actions, in his life":* These final passages in Siddhartha's teachings (which are, of course, not teachings) to Govinda show the combination of Hesse's intellectual preference for the unity vision of the monistic Vedist insight and his emotional preference for the more complex integration of nonduality. They show the supremacy of love over wisdom conceived as a departure from the human. Siddhartha even has Govinda here repeat an understanding of the Buddha's teaching that states that it could never include love, only benevolence, sympathy, and so on. But then Siddhartha and Hesse contradict that interpretation, call it a misunderstanding, and insist on the presence of a Mahayana universalism in the Buddha's body and life, if not in the words known in those days only from the Theravada Pali

sources. This deep prescience of Hesse, lacking in his day any sources that would have conveyed this insight to him, is truly marvelous.

17. (p. 118) *This, Govinda knew, was how the Perfect Ones smiled.*: In the very end, in Govinda's vision, the two Siddharthas are united. As the historical (or mythical) Siddhartha becomes the Buddha, and Hesse's inner Buddha becomes Siddhartha, Govinda experiences and deeply understands them to be one and the same. Govinda himself here resembles the Buddha's close disciple Ananda, who was the closest attendant of the Buddha and yet failed to attain enlightenment while the Buddha lived, being so preoccupied with serving his teacher. Within a week or two of the Buddha's passing away, however, Ananda was thrown back on himself by the shock of the loss, and soon he became fully enlightened and shortly thereafter assumed the responsibility as the head of the community.

# Inspired by
# SIDDHARTHA

Hermann Hesse wrote *Siddhartha* in 1922 and won the Nobel Prize for Literature in 1946. But it was not until 1951 that Hesse's novel of enlightenment was translated into English. *Siddhartha* was published by the legendary house New Directions, founded in 1936 by poet James Laughlin. New Directions—which brought neglected authors such as F. Scott Fitzgerald and Henry James back into the canon—printed the volume at the urging of author Henry Miller, who considered it a way out of what he called the "air-conditioned nightmare" of America. Financed almost entirely by Laughlin, *Siddhartha* became the book that made the fifteen-year-old publishing house profitable.

One of the most widely read books of the twentieth century, *Siddhartha* began amassing its monumental following among members of the 1960s counterculture. Siddhartha's struggle to find contentment dovetailed perfectly with the feelings of restlessness and discontent experienced by that young, rebellious generation. As young people increasingly disavowed bourgeois values and expressed intense feelings of alienation and a growing interest in Eastern spiritualism, many saw *Siddhartha* as the text that precisely recorded their emotions and captured the zeitgeist of the sixties.

*On the Road* (1957), by Jack Kerouac, is often seen as a spiritual companion text to *Siddhartha*. Like its predecessor, *On the Road* appeared in America in the 1950s and took hold strongly in the following decade. The novel's largely autobiographical narrator, Sal Paradise, finished with college and immensely unfulfilled, embarks on a whirlwind, drug-induced road trip across America with his pal and former jailbird Dean Moriarty (based on Kerouac's friend Neal Cassady). As *Siddhartha* sprang from Hesse's three-month trek through Indonesia, Malaysia, and Ceylon in 1911, Kerouac was inspired to write *On the Road*—nearly without stopping—after his own journey across America. Seen as a seminal text of the Beat generation, *On the Road* acquired a following as wide as that of *Siddhartha*. In fact, it is no coincidence that after publishing *Siddhartha*, New Directions was influential in cultivating and printing numerous Beat writers, including Allen Ginsberg, Lawrence Ferlinghetti, and Kerouac himself.

Other works by Hesse—most notably *Steppenwolf* (1927)—were also among the most popular literature of the 1960s. *Steppenwolf* tells the story of Henry Haller, the title character, from three points of view. The Steppenwolf came to be seen as the outsider in society, the artist or intellectual whose struggle against middle-class conformity is matched only by an interior struggle against loneliness. Harvard professor turned LSD-guru Timothy Leary called the book a "psychedelic trip" and named Hesse "a poet of the interior journey." Allusions to mind-altering substances in *Steppenwolf* and *On the Road* may have added to their appeal; more important, these novels are significant for delineating a search for meaning in America—a society that seemed to place convenience, wealth, and comfort above spirituality.

# COMMENTS & QUESTIONS

*In this section, we aim to provide the reader with an array of perspectives on the text, as well as questions that challenge those perspectives. The commentary has been culled from sources as diverse as reviews contemporaneous with the work, letters written by the author, literary criticism of later generations, and appreciations written throughout the work's history. Following the commentary, a series of questions seeks to filter Hermann Hesse's* Siddhartha *through a variety of points of view and bring about a richer understanding of this enduring work.*

## Comments

### FREDERICK MORGAN

Hermann Hesse's *Siddhartha* is an example of a particular type of fiction that has long been a temptation to European writers with "poetic" temperaments. Stories written within this convention have an exotic setting; the action centers on the hero's "quest for Truth" through different ways of life; the style tends to be high-flown, and the "Truth" finally attained is usually found to reside in the blurred, orientally-inspired pseudo-mysticism of "acceptance" and "affirmation," so dear to our Jungians and other fuzzy thinkers. *Siddhartha* follows the pattern: for all the competence of the writing and the construction, it lacks both intellectual grasp and emotional truth. The style is merely decorative, "poetic" in the bad sense, lacking a real object; the book as a whole, without roots in real experience, seems to me, for all its superficial elegance, finally trivial.

—from *Hudson Review* (Spring 1952)

### KARL S. WEIMAR

*Siddhartha* introduces the English reader to that non-Western component of Hesse's Weltanschauung, his mystical realism, which leads him to experience aesthetically and immediately the all-embracing, undifferentiated, indeterminate continuum. Only now can the English reader appreciate the unique coexistence of Eastern and Western philosophies in Hesse's work.

—from *German Quarterly* (November 1953)

BERNARD LANDIS

*Siddhartha* contains all of the fundamentals of Hesse's philosophy: the division of the universe into masculine and feminine worlds, the cult of suffering, anathema of dogma, antipathy to group action, the concept of the garden-forest as a source of security, and the everlasting conflict of new against old, birth against death, in the recurring life cycle.

—from *Accent* (Winter 1953)

THEODORE ZIOLKOWSKI

Hesse's attitude toward the East is at this time not one of enthusiastic affirmation, but rather of critical assessment. The magic of the East, which he clearly regards as an image of a lost and irrecoverable paradise, exerts an ineluctable attraction upon his mind and imagination, and he returns to it again and again. Yet he pores over the lore and wisdom of the East with a skeptical eye, striving to single out those elements that are relevant to his own problems and, in turn, testing and sharpening his own thoughts on the systems that he discovers there. This is particularly evident in his journals from the year 1920, precisely during the composition of *Siddhartha*.

"My preoccupation with India, which has been going on for almost twenty years and has passed through many stages, now seems to me to have reached a new point of development. Previously my reading, searching and sympathies were restricted exclusively to the philosophical aspect of India—the purely intellectual, Vedantic and Buddhistic aspect. The Upanishads, the sayings of Buddha, and the Bhagavad Gita were the focal point of this world. Only recently have I been approaching the actual religious India of the gods, of Vishnu and Indra, Brahma and Krishna. And now Buddhism appears to me more and more as a kind of very pure, highly bred reformation—a purification and spiritualization that has no flaw but its great zeal-ousness, with which it destroys image-worlds for which it can offer no replacement."

—from *The Novels of Hermann Hesse* (1965)

## Questions

1. Bernard Landis speaks of Hesse's philosophy as inclusive of masculine and feminine worlds. Which does Siddhartha belong to, or does he vacillate between the two? Is Siddhartha androg-ynous?

2. In a letter, Hesse once wrote: "The call of death is a call of love. Death can be sweet if we answer it in the affirmative, if we ac-cept it as one of the great eternal forms of life and transforma-tion." Elsewhere, Hesse wrote: "I cannot rid myself of the idea that instead of Death with his scythe, it will be my mother who takes me to herself once more and leads me back into non-exis-tence and innocence." Hesse's optimism surrounding death may account, in part, for his unfaltering popularity. How does *Sid-dhartha* address death? Do Siddhartha's own transformations in life correspond to the reincarnation cycle, or is each new step a preparation for "the call of death"?

3. The philosophy of *Siddhartha* is a healthful counterbalance to the Western way of living and seeing. Would you say that this statement is true or false?

4. Can one abstract from *Siddhartha* a clear, concisely formu-lated message? Would the world be a better place if everybody accepted the worldview or religion or philosophy revealed at the end of *Siddhartha*?

5. Do you prefer any of Siddhartha's stages that precede his final stage of enlightenment? That is, would you be satisfied not mak-ing it to the end of the journey? Why?

6. Do you feel that, on the whole, such matters as ambition, sexual desire, and pleasure in the things of this world are good or bad?

7. What would you have to give up in order to live as *Siddhartha* seems to recommend?

# FOR FURTHER READING

### *Other Works by Hermann Hesse*

*Peter Camenzind*, 1904

*Unterm Rad (Beneath the Wheel)*, 1906

*Gertrud (Gertrude)*, 1910

*Rosshalde*, 1914

*Demian*, 1919

*Der Steppenwolf (Steppenwolf)*, 1927

*Narziss und Goldmund (Narcissus and Goldmund)*, 1930

*Die Morgenlandfahrt (The Journey to the East)*, 1932

*Das Glasperlenspiel (The Glass Bead Game)*, 1943

### *Books Worth Reading to Deepen Appreciation of* Siddhartha

Armstrong, Karen. *Buddha*. Penguin Lives Series. New York: Viking, 2001.

Cleary, Thomas, trans. *The Flower Ornament Scripture*. Boston: Shambhala, 1993.

Conze, Edward, trans. *The Perfection of Wisdom in Eight Thousand Lines & Its Verse Summary*. Bolinas, CA: Four Seasons Foundation, 1973; distributed by Book People, Berkeley, CA.

Dalai Lama, with Howard C. Cutler. *The Art of Happiness: A Handbook for Living*. New York: Riverhead Books, 1998.

Dowman, Keith, trans. *Masters of Mahamudra: Songs and Histories of the Eighty-four Buddhist Siddhas*. SUNY Series in Buddhist Studies. Albany, NY: State University of New York Press, 1985.

Fields, Rick. *How the Swans Came to the Lake: A Narrative History of Buddhism in America*. Boston: Shambhala, 1992.

Lhalungpa, Lobsang, trans. *The Life of Milarepa.* Boulder: Shambhala, 1979.

Murcott, Susan. *The First Buddhist Women: Translations and Commentaries on the Therigatha.* Berkeley, CA: Parallax Press, 1991.

Olivelle, Patrick. *Upanishads.* New York: Oxford University Press, 1996.

Rabten, Geshé. *Echoes of Voidness.* London: Wisdom Publications, 1983.

Rahula, Walpola. *What the Buddha Taught.* New York: Grove Press, 1974.

Shantideva. *The Way of the Bodhisattva: A Translation of the Bodhicharyavatara.* Translated by the Padmakara Translation Group. Boston: Shambhala, 1997.

Thich Nhat Hanh. *Being Peace.* Edited by Arnold Kotler. Berkeley, CA: Parallax Press, 1987.

Thurman, Robert A. F., trans. *The Central Philosophy of Tibet: A Study and Translation of Jey Tsong Khapa's* Essence of True Eloquence. Foreword by the Dalai Lama. Princeton, NJ: Princeton University Press, 1984.

———. *The Holy Teaching of Vimalakirti: A Mahayana Scripture.* University Park: Pennsylvania State University Press, 1976.

Thurman, Robert A. F. *Infinite Life: Seven Virtues for Living Well.* Foreword by the Dalai Lama. New York: Riverhead Books, 2004.

———. *Inner Revolution: Life, Liberty, and the Pursuit of Real Happiness.* Foreword by the Dalai Lama. New York: Riverhead Books, 1998.

Walshe, Maurice, trans. *The Long Discourses of the Buddha: A Translation of the Digha Nikaya.* Boston: Wisdom Publications, 1995.

Look for the following titles, available now from
## BARNES & NOBLE CLASSICS

Visit your local bookstore for these and more fine titles.
Or to order online go to: www.bn.com/classics

| | | | |
|---|---|---|---|
| Adventures of Huckleberry Finn | Mark Twain | 1-59308-112-X | $5.95 |
| The Adventures of Tom Sawyer | Mark Twain | 1-59308-139-1 | $5.95 |
| The Aeneid | Vergil | 1-59308-237-1 | $8.95 |
| Aesop's Fables | | 1-59308-062-X | $5.95 |
| The Age of Innocence | Edith Wharton | 1-59308-143-X | $5.95 |
| Agnes Grey | Anne Brontë | 1-59308-323-8 | $6.95 |
| Alice's Adventures in Wonderland and Through the Looking-Glass | Lewis Carroll | 1-59308-015-8 | $7.95 |
| The Ambassadors | Henry James | 1-59308-378-5 | $8.95 |
| Anna Karenina | Leo Tolstoy | 1-59308-027-1 | $8.95 |
| The Arabian Nights | Anonymous | 1-59308-281-9 | $9.95 |
| The Art of War | Sun Tzu | 1-59308-017-4 | $7.95 |
| The Autobiography of an Ex-Colored Man and Other Writings | James Weldon Johnson | 1-59308-289-4 | $5.95 |
| The Awakening and Selected Short Fiction | Kate Chopin | 1-59308-113-8 | $6.95 |
| Babbitt | Sinclair Lewis | 1-59308-267-3 | $8.95 |
| The Beautiful and Damned | F. Scott Fitzgerald | 1-59308-245-2 | $7.95 |
| Beowulf | Anonymous | 1-59308-266-5 | $6.95 |
| Billy Budd and The Piazza Tales | Herman Melville | 1-59308-253-3 | $6.95 |
| Bleak House | Charles Dickens | 1-59308-311-4 | $9.95 |
| The Bostonians | Henry James | 1-59308-297-5 | $8.95 |
| The Brothers Karamazov | Fyodor Dostoevsky | 1-59308-045-X | $9.95 |
| Bulfinch's Mythology | Thomas Bulfinch | 1-59308-273-8 | $12.95 |
| The Call of the Wild and White Fang | Jack London | 1-59308-200-2 | $5.95 |
| Candide | Voltaire | 1-59308-028-X | $6.95 |
| The Canterbury Tales | Geoffrey Chaucer | 1-59308-080-8 | $9.95 |
| A Christmas Carol, The Chimes and The Cricket on the Hearth | Charles Dickens | 1-59308-033-6 | $6.95 |
| The Collected Oscar Wilde | | 1-59308-310-6 | $9.95 |
| The Collected Poems of Emily Dickinson | | 1-59308-050-6 | $5.95 |
| Common Sense and Other Writings | Thomas Paine | 1-59308-209-6 | $6.95 |
| The Communist Manifesto and Other Writings | Karl Marx and Friedrich Engels | 1-59308-100-6 | $5.95 |
| The Complete Sherlock Holmes, Vol. I | Sir Arthur Conan Doyle | 1-59308-034-4 | $7.95 |
| The Complete Sherlock Holmes, Vol. II | Sir Arthur Conan Doyle | 1-59308-040-9 | $9.95 |
| Confessions | Saint Augustine | 1-59308-259-2 | $6.95 |
| A Connecticut Yankee in King Arthur's Court | Mark Twain | 1-59308-210-X | $7.95 |
| The Count of Monte Cristo | Alexandre Dumas | 1-59308-151-0 | $9.95 |
| The Country of the Pointed Firs and Selected Short Fiction | Sarah Orne Jewett | 1-59308-262-2 | $7.95 |
| Crime and Punishment | Fyodor Dostoevsky | 1-59308-081-6 | $8.95 |
| Cyrano de Bergerac | Edmond Rostand | 1-59308-387-4 | $7.95 |
| Daisy Miller and Washington Square | Henry James | 1-59308-105-7 | $5.95 |
| Daniel Deronda | George Eliot | 1-59308-290-8 | $9.95 |

(continued)

| | | | |
|---|---|---|---|
| **Dead Souls** | Nikolai Gogol | 1-59308-092-1 | $9.95 |
| **The Deerslayer** | James Fenimore Cooper | 1-59308-211-8 | $10.95 |
| **Don Quixote** | Miguel de Cervantes | 1-59308-046-8 | $9.95 |
| **Dracula** | Bram Stoker | 1-59308-114-6 | $6.95 |
| **Emma** | Jane Austen | 1-59308-152-9 | $6.95 |
| **Essays and Poems by Ralph Waldo Emerson** | | 1-59308-076-X | $6.95 |
| **Essential Dialogues of Plato** | | 1-59308-269-X | $10.95 |
| **The Essential Tales and Poems of Edgar Allan Poe** | | 1-59308-064-6 | $7.95 |
| **Ethan Frome and Selected Stories** | Edith Wharton | 1-59308-090-5 | $5.95 |
| **Fairy Tales** | Hans Christian Andersen | 1-59308-260-6 | $9.95 |
| **Far from the Madding Crowd** | Thomas Hardy | 1-59308-223-1 | $7.95 |
| **The Federalist** | Hamilton, Madison, Jay | 1-59308-282-7 | $7.95 |
| **Founding America: Documents from the Revolution to the Bill of Rights** | Jefferson, et al. | 1-59308-230-4 | $9.95 |
| **Frankenstein** | Mary Shelley | 1-59308-115-4 | $5.95 |
| **The Good Soldier** | Ford Madox Ford | 1-59308-268-1 | $7.95 |
| **Great American Short Stories: From Hawthorne to Hemingway** | Various | 1-59308-086-7 | $9.95 |
| **The Great Escapes: Four Slave Narratives** | Various | 1-59308-294-0 | $6.95 |
| **Great Expectations** | Charles Dickens | 1-59308-116-2 | $6.95 |
| **Grimm's Fairy Tales** | Jacob and Wilhelm Grimm | 1-59308-056-5 | $9.95 |
| **Gulliver's Travels** | Jonathan Swift | 1-59308-132-4 | $5.95 |
| **Hard Times** | Charles Dickens | 1-59308-156-1 | $5.95 |
| **Heart of Darkness and Selected Short Fiction** | Joseph Conrad | 1-59308-123-5 | $5.95 |
| **The History of the Peloponnesian War** | Thucydides | 1-59308-091-3 | $11.95 |
| **The House of Mirth** | Edith Wharton | 1-59308-153-7 | $7.95 |
| **The House of the Dead and Poor Folk** | Fyodor Dostoevsky | 1-59308-194-4 | $9.95 |
| **The House of the Seven Gables** | Nathaniel Hawthorne | 1-59308-231-2 | $7.95 |
| **The Hunchback of Notre Dame** | Victor Hugo | 1-59308-140-5 | $7.95 |
| **The Idiot** | Fyodor Dostoevsky | 1-59308-058-1 | $7.95 |
| **The Iliad** | Homer | 1-59308-232-0 | $8.95 |
| **The Importance of Being Earnest and Four Other Plays** | Oscar Wilde | 1-59308-059-X | $7.95 |
| **Incidents in the Life of a Slave Girl** | Harriet Jacobs | 1-59308-283-5 | $6.95 |
| **The Inferno** | Dante Alighieri | 1-59308-051-4 | $7.95 |
| **The Interpretation of Dreams** | Sigmund Freud | 1-59308-298-3 | $9.95 |
| **Ivanhoe** | Sir Walter Scott | 1-59308-246-0 | $9.95 |
| **Jane Eyre** | Charlotte Brontë | 1-59308-117-0 | $7.95 |
| **Journey to the Center of the Earth** | Jules Verne | 1-59308-252-5 | $4.95 |
| **Jude the Obscure** | Thomas Hardy | 1-59308-035-2 | $6.95 |
| **The Jungle Books** | Rudyard Kipling | 1-59308-109-X | $5.95 |
| **The Jungle** | Upton Sinclair | 1-59308-118-9 | $7.95 |
| **King Solomon's Mines** | H. Rider Haggard | 1-59308-275-4 | $7.95 |
| **Lady Chatterley's Lover** | D. H. Lawrence | 1-59308-239-8 | $7.95 |
| **The Last of the Mohicans** | James Fenimore Cooper | 1-59308-137-5 | $7.95 |
| **Leaves of Grass: First and "Death-bed" Editions** | Walt Whitman | 1-59308-083-2 | $11.95 |
| **The Legend of Sleepy Hollow and Other Writings** | Washington Irving | 1-59308-225-8 | $6.95 |
| **Les Misérables** | Victor Hugo | 1-59308-066-2 | $9.95 |
| **Les Liaisons Dangereuses** | Pierre Choderlos de Laclos | 1-59308-240-1 | $8.95 |
| **Little Women** | Louisa May Alcott | 1-59308-108-1 | $6.95 |

(continued)

| | | | |
|---|---|---|---|
| Lost Illusions | Honoré de Balzac | 1-59308-315-7 | $9.95 |
| Madame Bovary | Gustave Flaubert | 1-59308-052-2 | $6.95 |
| Maggie: A Girl of the Streets and Other Writings about New York | Stephen Crane | 1-59308-248-7 | $8.95 |
| The Magnificent Ambersons | Booth Tarkington | 1-59308-263-0 | $8.95 |
| Main Street | Sinclair Lewis | 1-59308-386-6 | $9.95 |
| Man and Superman and Three Other Plays | George Bernard Shaw | 1-59308-067-0 | $7.95 |
| The Man in the Iron Mask | Alexandre Dumas | 1-59308-233-9 | $10.95 |
| Mansfield Park | Jane Austen | 1-59308-154-5 | $5.95 |
| The Mayor of Casterbridge | Thomas Hardy | 1-59308-309-2 | $7.95 |
| The Metamorphoses | Ovid | 1-59308-276-2 | $7.95 |
| The Metamorphosis and Other Stories | Franz Kafka | 1-59308-029-8 | $6.95 |
| Moby-Dick | Herman Melville | 1-59308-018-2 | $9.95 |
| Moll Flanders | Daniel Defoe | 1-59308-216-9 | $8.95 |
| My Ántonia | Willa Cather | 1-59308-202-9 | $5.95 |
| My Bondage and My Freedom | Frederick Douglass | 1-59308-301-7 | $8.95 |
| Narrative of Sojourner Truth | | 1-59308-293-2 | $6.95 |
| Narrative of the Life of Frederick Douglass, an American Slave | | 1-59308-041-7 | $4.95 |
| Nicholas Nickleby | Charles Dickens | 1-59308-300-9 | $8.95 |
| Night and Day | Virginia Woolf | 1-59308-212-6 | $9.95 |
| Nostromo | Joseph Conrad | 1-59308-193-6 | $9.95 |
| Notes from Underground, The Double and Other Stories | Fyodor Dostoevsky | 1-59308-124-3 | $9.95 |
| O Pioneers! | Willa Cather | 1-59308-205-3 | $5.95 |
| The Odyssey | Homer | 1-59308-009-3 | $5.95 |
| Of Human Bondage | W. Somerset Maugham | 1-59308-238-X | $10.95 |
| Oliver Twist | Charles Dickens | 1-59308-206-1 | $6.95 |
| The Origin of Species | Charles Darwin | 1-59308-077-8 | $7.95 |
| Paradise Lost | John Milton | 1-59308-095-6 | $8.95 |
| The Paradiso | Dante Alighieri | 1-59308-317-3 | $9.95 |
| Père Goriot | Honoré de Balzac | 1-59308-285-1 | $8.95 |
| Persuasion | Jane Austen | 1-59308-130-8 | $5.95 |
| Peter Pan | J. M. Barrie | 1-59308-213-4 | $4.95 |
| The Phantom of the Opera | Gaston Leroux | 1-59308-249-5 | $6.95 |
| The Picture of Dorian Gray | Oscar Wilde | 1-59308-025-5 | $5.95 |
| The Pilgrim's Progress | John Bunyan | 1-59308-254-1 | $7.95 |
| A Portrait of the Artist as a Young Man and Dubliners | James Joyce | 1-59308-031-X | $7.95 |
| The Possessed | Fyodor Dostoevsky | 1-59308-250-9 | $10.95 |
| Pride and Prejudice | Jane Austen | 1-59308-201-0 | $6.95 |
| The Prince and Other Writings | Niccolò Machiavelli | 1-59308-060-3 | $5.95 |
| The Prince and the Pauper | Mark Twain | 1-59308-218-5 | $4.95 |
| Pudd'nhead Wilson and Those Extraordinary Twins | Mark Twain | 1-59308-255-X | $7.95 |
| The Purgatorio | Dante Alighieri | 1-59308-219-3 | $9.95 |
| Pygmalion and Three Other Plays | George Bernard Shaw | 1-59308-078-6 | $8.95 |
| The Red Badge of Courage and Selected Short Fiction | Stephen Crane | 1-59308-119-7 | $4.95 |
| Republic | Plato | 1-59308-097-2 | $7.95 |
| The Return of the Native | Thomas Hardy | 1-59308-220-7 | $7.95 |
| Robinson Crusoe | Daniel Defoe | 1-59308-360-2 | $5.95 |
| A Room with a View | E. M. Forster | 1-59308-288-6 | $7.95 |
| Scaramouche | Rafael Sabatini | 1-59308-242-8 | $9.95 |
| The Scarlet Letter | Nathaniel Hawthorne | 1-59308-207-X | $5.95 |

(continued)

| | | | |
|---|---|---|---|
| The Scarlet Pimpernel | Baroness Orczy | 1-59308-234-7 | $5.95 |
| The Secret Agent | Joseph Conrad | 1-59308-305-X | $8.95 |
| The Secret Garden | Frances Hodgson Burnett | 1-59308-277-0 | $5.95 |
| Selected Stories of O. Henry | | 1-59308-042-5 | $5.95 |
| Sense and Sensibility | Jane Austen | 1-59308-125-1 | $5.95 |
| Siddhartha | Hermann Hesse | 1-59308-379-3 | $6.95 |
| Silas Marner and Two Short Stories | George Eliot | 1-59308-251-7 | $6.95 |
| Sister Carrie | Theodore Dreiser | 1-59308-226-6 | $10.95 |
| The Souls of Black Folk | W. E. B. Du Bois | 1-59308-014-X | $5.95 |
| The Strange Case of Dr. Jekyll and Mr. Hyde and Other Stories | Robert Louis Stevenson | 1-59308-131-6 | $5.95 |
| Swann's Way | Marcel Proust | 1-59308-295-9 | $9.95 |
| A Tale of Two Cities | Charles Dickens | 1-59308-138-3 | $5.95 |
| Tarzan of the Apes | Edgar Rice Burroughs | 1-59308-227-4 | $7.95 |
| Tess of d'Urbervilles | Thomas Hardy | 1-59308-228-2 | $7.95 |
| This Side of Paradise | F. Scott Fitzgerald | 1-59308-243-6 | $7.95 |
| Three Theban Plays | Sophocles | 1-59308-235-5 | $7.95 |
| Thus Spoke Zarathustra | Friedrich Nietzsche | 1-59308-278-9 | $7.95 |
| The Time Machine and The Invisible Man | H. G. Wells | 1-59308-388-2 | $6.95 |
| Tom Jones | Henry Fielding | 1-59308-070-0 | $8.95 |
| Treasure Island | Robert Louis Stevenson | 1-59308-247-9 | $4.95 |
| The Turn of the Screw, The Aspern Papers and Two Stories | Henry James | 1-59308-043-3 | $5.95 |
| Twenty Thousand Leagues Under the Sea | Jules Verne | 1-59308-302-5 | $5.95 |
| Uncle Tom's Cabin | Harriet Beecher Stowe | 1-59308-121-9 | $7.95 |
| Vanity Fair | William Makepeace Thackeray | 1-59308-071-9 | $7.95 |
| The Varieties of Religious Experience | William James | 1-59308-072-7 | $9.95 |
| Villette | Charlotte Brontë | 1-59308-316-5 | $9.95 |
| The Virginian | Owen Wister | 1-59308-236-3 | $9.95 |
| Walden and Civil Disobedience | Henry David Thoreau | 1-59308-208-8 | $6.95 |
| War and Peace | Leo Tolstoy | 1-59308-073-5 | $12.95 |
| The War of the Worlds | H. G. Wells | 1-59308-362-9 | $5.95 |
| Ward No. 6 and Other Stories | Anton Chekhov | 1-59308-003-4 | $7.95 |
| The Waste Land and Other Poems | T. S. Eliot | 1-59308-279-7 | $4.95 |
| The Way We Live Now | Anthony Trollope | 1-59308-304-1 | $12.95 |
| The Wind in the Willows | Kenneth Grahame | 1-59308-265-7 | $6.95 |
| The Wings of the Dove | Henry James | 1-59308-296-7 | $9.95 |
| Wives and Daughters | Elizabeth Gaskell | 1-59308-257-6 | $7.95 |
| The Woman in White | Wilkie Collins | 1-59308-280-0 | $7.95 |
| Women in Love | D. H. Lawrence | 1-59308-258-4 | $9.95 |
| The Wonderful Wizard of Oz | L. Frank Baum | 1-59308-221-5 | $6.95 |
| Wuthering Heights | Emily Brontë | 1-59308-128-6 | $5.95 |

## BARNES & NOBLE CLASSICS

If you are an educator and would like to receive an
Examination or Desk Copy of a Barnes & Noble Classics edition,
please refer to Academic Resources on our website at
WWW.BN.COM/CLASSICS
or contact us at
BNCLASSICS@BN.COM

All prices are subject to change.